TRUTH, LIES, AND DECEIT

| ALSO BY NELSON COVER |

Danced by the Light of the Moon

THE SESSIONS UNIVERSITY SERIES
From the Midst of Wickedness
A Matter of Circumstance

TRUTH, LIES, AND DECEIT

Stories

NELSON COVER

Epigraph Books
Rhinebeck, New York

Truth, Lies, and Deceit: Stories © 2021 by Nelson Cover

Paperback ISBN 978-1-954744-42-4
Hardcover ISBN 978-1-954744-43-1
eBook ISBN 978-1-954744-44-8

Library of Congress Control Number 2021919317

Book design by Colin Rolfe

Epigraph Books
22 East Market Street, Suite 304
Rhinebeck, NY 12572
(845) 876-4861
epigraphps.com

Contents

Foreword

People are often fascinated by the mystery of the creative process. It surprises them that in many cases so too are authors.

For instance, for every short story in this collection inspired by an event or multiple events in life, there is another whose genesis was entirely unanticipated, like *Zoltan's Lie*, where its principal characters, its setting and its plot came out of nowhere and where its characters became such close imaginary friends that I was encouraged to follow them through *From the Midst of Wickedness*, the first Sessions University novel, and then again through its sequel, *A Matter of Circumstance*. In fact, Thomas and Zoltan are such pests that they are becoming embroiled yet again in a third novel where, as usual, I am somewhat cluelessly following their lead.

But to the prospective reader's more important question: Why should I read this collection? For starters, entertainment. For the payoff, enlightenment.

I have been blessed in my life and my career to have close relationships with fascinating people whose attributes were often as great as their flaws. In the creative process their inspiration and their stories or parts of them form an amalgamation of life lessons where characters take on certain physical and personality traits out of a quiver of potentialities to create a whole new being and where plots are derived and melded together from experiences to form a parallel universe.

The fact is, each of our lives, whether we care to admit it or not, are inevitably tied up in a Gordian knot of truth, lies and deceit. Hopefully, then, this collection helps the reader see and better understand their own reality as reflected in the fiction which follows.

Hello George

The notion is that I am enjoying a late-night drive, the drive one takes to clear the mind, reflect, to think about and work out life's issues and problems. Except... it dawns on me slowly, at first dream-like, that I'm not reflecting about anything at all.

I am driving.

On a highway.

Very late at night or very early in the morning.

The first clue that something is wrong: I do not know where I am.

A sinking feeling splashed with a spasm of panic runs through me, demanding accountability. I put my mind into overdrive for recall. Nothing. Headache, stomach a mess, the end of my nose a bit numb, the beginnings of a terrible hangover. All the signs are there. I am... how can one say this adroitly? Shitfaced. How the hell can I drive when I am this drunk? Okay, do not want to know. I'll take it. Look at the speedometer. Going 45 miles per hour. A speed limit sign pops up. 65 mile an hour speed limit. Oops. Accelerate. Driving in a straight line. Something to be said for that. Something weird about the speedometer. What?

Look around, slowly, carefully. Clues.... Please!

Driving a brand-new black Cadillac Escalade with a beautiful tan leather interior so fragrant I want to puke. 4,510 miles on the speedometer.

Car's stereo blasting woebegone country music.

Hate country music.

I reach over while keeping my eyes on the road, fumble around and turned it off.

Something not right about the sound system's controls, location, graphics. Come back to that.

Dashboard clock says 2:17am.

Brenda will be so pissed. Never happened before, but to a wife and newly appointed board member of the National Council for Substance Abuse Prevention this situation and whatever other details it might contain... Come back to that.

Something not right about the dashboard clock too. Come back to that.

Where the hell am I?

Hundreds of high-pressure sodium lights make the surroundings seem clinically dead yet blindingly intense.

There is a major highway to the right separated by a heavy guard rail. To the left is a wide expanse of oncoming lanes and beyond modern office buildings with tech names on them.

No exits in sight.

I know this road.

I think hard and finally it dawns on me that I am on the Dulles Airport Access Road, a no toll, no exit almost 14-mile highway to and from Dulles Airport. A sign appears conveniently telling me that it is 6 miles to the airport.

I think for a while longer, then smile momentarily.

No, I am sure I am not on some dumb ass errand for my boss, the senator. No one to pick up at the airport. As for getting home, I am headed in the opposite direction from where Brenda and I live in Silver Spring, Maryland. She is going to be so pissed.

The stereo system and clock resurface as concerns.

We own a ten-year-old green Ford Explorer.

I hear an inhalation filled with stark horror. My own.

This is not our car! Yet somewhere deep in my consciousness it dawns on me that I have seen this car I am driving before. In fact, I have ridden in it.

I let out a girlish scream. This is the senator's new car. He loves this car. Around the office he calls it his "Escapade" which always gets a chuckle from the support staff, ass kissers one and all. But the fact is that it is his pride and joy, with the license plates personalized to spell out his state's football team's name without the vowels.

Ohhhh, shit! What the hell am I doing in his car?

A jumble of recollections begins flashing randomly.

Brenda and I on R Street in Georgetown where we parked our Explorer a block away from the Redfern's house. Mid-November chill, some trees, protected from the worst weather and wind by the surrounding townhouses, still dropping their leaves casually, the culverts piled high with them, wet yellow and crimson, the dusky scent of them in the air as we confronted one another.

"John, you can't drive," she tells me.

"Suurre I can," I hear myself slur.

I reach into my blazer pocket and pull out my keys. They slide from my hand without inhibition and hit the sidewalk with a crisp metallic sound.

I look at the keys. Look at Brenda. Look at the keys.

"Youuu drive," I say reasonably.

She leans over, snatches the keys from the sidewalk, walks angrily around the car, gets in, starts it and while I watch, with a few maneuvers, pulls out into the street and drives away.

I think back to the Redfern's party, a victory party to celebrate the senator's successful reelection the week before.

Their large four-story Federal townhouse is one of their five homes but they spend a good deal of time here as Sam and Mrs. Redfern, Ellie, envision themselves as patriots and love rubbing elbows in the mixing bowl of Washington, DC's social arena which includes all their fellow patriots on the make, congressmen and senators and their wives, policy wonks, non-profit CEOs, business leaders and lobbyists, a few Hollywood types.

The Redferns had made quite a splash over the last several years, spending prodigiously to support local causes and their elected representatives in Maryland. Sam's a developer who founded his company in Reisterstown and has expanded to now have projects throughout the United States and abroad. In wealth parlance he might be called the billionaire next door.

Naturally, it was in the senator's, Leonard Faulkner, and his wife, Marguerite's interest to become close friends with Sam and Ellie. As administrative assistant to Senator, I was just part of the friendship, their humble servant.

Brenda was already pissed at having to accompany me to the party. Working for an environmental policy organization, she felt superior to this crowd, had in fact voted for the other party in the last election. She, after all, was about saving humanity, not serving blind ambition. She tolerated my life and employment on the Hill, but that did not mean she wanted to be part of it. Just the opposite.

I had had very little sleep over the last few weeks helping to pull out every stop to assure the senator's victory and then begin the unwinding process. It had been a crazy time during which my absence and overextension just stoked Brenda's resentment.

We were punctual of course, early even because we made extra time to find a parking spot in Georgetown, an increasingly impossible task, but damned if someone did not actually pull out of one just as we reached the spot.

Sam and Ellie were at the door greeting everyone, the Faulkners next in line, to say hello and receive congratulations.

Sam was an energetic fire plug of a man, almost as wide as he was tall, a man who liked his bourbon, red faced to the point you wished someone would slap a blood pressure cuff on his left arm and ask him to sit down, a hail-fellow-well-met, direct, profane, at times hilarious, at other times way over the top in the polite, politically correct and utterly insincere world of Washington, DC. He was wearing a store bought big and tall suit without tailoring and I knew one thing for certain, Sam did not care about his appearance or what others thought of it. He had succeeded in life by bulldozing his way over obstacles.

Ellie was a dear, sweet, innocent who believed in Sam, God and her country, who tried with all her might to dress the part of Washington but where something was always a bit off. Tonight she was inexpertly hobbling in high heels, dressed in the latest from the Wisconsin Avenue fashion stores. When around Ellie, she reminded me of Minnie Pearl and her straw hat with the price tag dangling from it.

The house was elegantly and tastefully furnished with a mix of antiquities, textiles, sculptures and paintings brought in by their interior decorator but somehow, despite all the elegant décor, it felt like a hotel. Store bought.

"Hey, young man," Sam greeted me, "I hope this slave driver to my right hasn't been workin' you too hard."

I replied, "Actually..." and just let it hang there. My comment plus what I knew was my well-deserved appearance of exhaustion was enough to cause everyone to chuckle, except Brenda.

Ellie gave me a hug and held my hand in both hers, said to Brenda, "We're so proud of what John and his fellow workers have accomplished for the senator." And then to me, "You were the backbone of this whole success."

"Thanks," I told her, wishing she would let go of my hand and watching Brenda out of the corner of my eye fake pleasant approval and appreciation of Ellie's remark.

"But, you know, the senator and his appeal to the people makes it a lot easier for us."

"So, true," Ellie remarked, "but you still deserve so much credit. We're so proud of you."

We moved onto the senator and Marguerite as other guests came in behind us, me chuckling to myself over Brenda having to fake wifely adoration at my being praised.

The senator gave me his typical iron handshake, put an arm around me and pulled me in. "Damned if we didn't do it, buddy," he told me, which was the same thing he had said to me last week. Turning to Marguerite, "What Ellie says goes triple for me." Then back to me, "You are a truly invaluable member of our team, John," while Marguerite nodded in agreement.

I resisted the impulse to mimic sticking my finger down my throat.

Marguerite said to Brenda, "You're so good to let us have John for this campaign. I'm sure it's been disruptive. Now we can all get on with our lives."

"Thankfully," Brenda commented.

We moved on, entering the living room and immediately ran into Ben Heartfield and his wife, Claire.

"Hey, buddy," Ben greeted, smirking, "You look as bad as I feel."

"Yeah, hazard of the profession." He truly did look exhausted.

Ben had moved over from his position as legislative assistant to run the Senator's campaign and had performed brilliantly. He would now move back to his former position.

Claire was in some ways a clone of Brenda, holding a high-ranking position with the World Wildlife Fund. Needless to say, they were delighted to see one another and quickly left Ben and I to our own devices, always a big mistake.

Ben and I had rarely seen one another over the past few weeks so after grabbing glasses of a fine Pinot Noir and small plates of hors d'oeuvres we began wandering around the house catching up with one another on various happenings during the campaign and after, blind luck successes, cluster fucks, bizarre behaviors, infighting, jousting and mudwrestling galore, the total circus of a political campaign.

Out back past the expansive brick patio a band was playing despite the cold weather, a dissipated group of old guys in 60s clothes, black leather jackets, sneakers, bowling shirts, peg pants. A few couples were dancing to the 60s rock and roll tunes under a small tent and dance floor. Dion's The Wanderer. Not a half bad rendition.

Since no one would seem to mind, we headed upstairs to explore the second and third floors. On the second we glanced in at the Redfern's palatial master suite. The third floor revealed a series of small suites and storage rooms and was heavy with the scent of marijuana.

Opening the most suspect door, we discovered several of the wait staff enjoying their break, passing a blunt around.

"Hey, hey, hey," said Ben looking at me.

I shrugged.

Invited to partake, we did in fact, unlike Bill Clinton, or probably just like him, inhale. I could feel my muscles unbinding as we took another hit. Maybe life was okay after all.

So it was that awhile later, having left our mellow friends on the third floor, we wandered, fatefully, into the Redfern's gourmet, multi-hundreds of thousands of dollars kitchen where in the back there was a long stainless-steel rolling table on which was set a buffet of crackers and cheese, a selection of well-aged bottles of bourbon with accompanying shot glasses.

Around the table stood other guests, some of whom I recognized and some I did not. Among them was a little old, sweet, elfin, red-faced man with whisps of white hair who I learned over time as we sipped and compared and stuffed our faces with crumbles of aged sharp cheddar cheese, brie and other fromage and crackers was Ellie Redfern's father, Leo.

The mood was festive and collegial, driven by our collective feeling of six more years of employment and career advancement.

And then Leo came around the table and stepped between Ben and me.

We discussed the merits of the different bourbons and after a time of great jocularity, Leo asked, "Have you met Gee-yorge?"

"No, who's George?" I inquired, hearing my voice coming out a bit slurry and looking around at the room, feeling almost clairvoyant as the room had powerfully and pleasantly shifted into crystalline focus.

"Ah," Leo said. "Come with me."

We followed him to a nearby door which he opened and clicked on a light. We found ourselves descending into a very large basement with a game room with a bar, home theatre, workout center, offices. We wound through the place until we reached a small, unfinished area in the back where a small ladder was propped against the studs flanking a brick wall.

"Hold my drink," Leo said.

"Sure."

He opened the ladder, climbed up two of its steps, reached up into the rafters and pulled down a bottle of George Dickel 17 Year Old Reserve.

"Meet Gee-yorge," he smiled at us and filled our glasses.

Then... darkness.

A picture flashes in my mind suddenly – a view of the front of the Redfern's house. Beside the dual limestone stairs and wrought iron railing is the entrance to their garage and parked there is the senator's new Escalade, which must have had the keys in the ignition.

Just like that, grand theft auto, gone in sixty seconds. What the hell was I thinking? Well, nothing, obviously. If only Angelina Jolie had been my shotgun babe.... Not funny. I am in a pigsty full of shit.

Ok. Anxiety! Fight it! Plan!

Obviously by now the senator and Mrs. Faulkner have probably reported the car to the police as stolen. And here I am driving it, practically the only car on the road, sticking out like big new shiny black sore thumb.

Fast. I had to get back to the Redferns, find a way to deposit the car someplace nearby without getting caught, wipe it down and get a cab home.

It was for these kinds of situations that cell phones were invented.

I pulled out my phone and after making the loop past the airport terminal and heading back into the District, tried not weave excessively while mapping the route from my current location back to the Redferns' address.

I called a cab to meet me there and damned if the same spot was still open in front of the the garage. Wiping the car down with my necktie only took a few minutes.

* * *

"How could you do this to me?"

Brenda's voice was beyond loud. It was the voice of an offended God, Zuul perhaps, primordial in its depth of emptiness and anger, descending from the heavens or perhaps from hell, jack hammering at my ears.

She was dressed in jeans and a smock.

Her faced was screwed up with anger and her honey brown hair swirled about as she yelled at me. Even in my misery a small part of what remained of my brain registered a thumb's up of approval of her looks. Telling her that her anger only made her look more beautiful was definitely not the right comment to make at this particular moment.

The kitchen clock told me that the time was a little after noon.

At least she had let me sleep.

I sat at our oak kitchen table, my head in my hands, searing, ice pick pain coming from behind my eyeballs. A piece of toast and jam pulsated nauseously in front of me, the offensive odor of my cup of coffee burned in my nose.

"Do you think you'll even have a job come Monday?" An incredulous shout.

"Why do you say that?" a voice sounding vaguely like mine responded.

"You don't remember? You don't know why I left?"

"No."

"You were sitting on a bench on the patio and a bunch of your staff and guests were dancing and you reached out and grabbed one of the interns. Grabbed her by her belt buckle and pulled her over onto you and you were both rolling around on the bricks. You don't remember any of that?"

"No." I had wondered why there was grit and sand all over my blazer. It definitely sounded as if I would not have a job tomorrow. I imagined being called into the senator's office, what might be said. No, the senator would never do things that way. He would have some else do his dirty work. Ben. God, that would be painful. Probably for both of us. I tamped down an upwelling of tears.

"Everyone there was trashed, including the senator and Marguerite, the Redferns, Ellie's father, Ben, everyone. Ellie's high heel caught in the patio bricks and she broke her ankle."

"Her father is how I got into trouble in the first place."

"How'd you get home?"

"Cab."

"You think I'm going to support you without a job? Is that what you think?"

I rummaged around in my consciousness and found it resembling a room post-robbery, all the drawers had been dumped on the floor and the furniture overturned.

I could not come up with a response.

Pain.

"I'm going out..." I said, composing myself, "to the patio."

"Why?"

"To think."

Brenda looked at me as if I had lost my mind.

I rose slowly, went to our front closet and put on my winter jacket, then shuffled to the patio's glass door, opened it and stepped outside. The air was humid and cold. An overcast day. I closed the door behind me.

We had planted an herbaceous border around the small flagstone patio enclosed by a wood basket weave privacy fence. Slowly I lowered myself onto one of the green plastic chairs, placed head in my hands and focused on the different bad sensations emanating from my body.

I heard myself groan.

* * *

The next morning I passed through security at the Hart Office Building without a hitch, which I viewed as a possible positive sign. That was enough to hold off my thinking that I should see the senator first thing and apologize for my behavior, throw myself upon his mercy.

All was normal in the office. No sign that anything was amiss. Finally, I wandered down the hall to Ben's office.

"Hey, howaryou doin'?"

Ben sat behind his desk which was piled high with papers. He looked terrible.

"Still recovering."

"Ohhh, don't I know."

"What the hell happened after Leo?"

"I don't have a clue. I was hoping you could tell me."

"Nope. All a big blank. First time that's ever happened to me."

"Hmph... Brenda told me that literally everybody who stayed was totally smacked."

"I guess. Claire was a mess. Called in sick today."

"Wow..." I began to have a surge of joyous revelation. Could it be possible that no one remembered the last hours of the party? No. Couldn't be. Yet, I had no idea how drunk the intern might have been when I had pulled her down onto the brick patio. Maybe Brenda was the only one sober.

"So," Ben said, "I've made a decision."

"Yeah?"

"I'm outta here by the end of next month."

"Nooo. Why?"

He placed his fingers together. "Can't stand this place

any longer. It's all wrong. Everything about it. We're supposed to be helping our constituents but the real deal is all we do is try to help ourselves and get reelected. There need to be sweeping changes. The whole system is compromised and corrupt, morally bankrupt."

"Whater you going to do?" I asked, incredulous.

"Oh, Claire's family owns a financial planning firm in her hometown near Sarasota. I'm going to join them. In a couple years I'll be back to the same income level with no state sales tax and a much lower cost of living. The kids will like it there, no winter, friendly, family oriented, still some sincerity left."

"Wow. I can't believe you're doing this."

"Believe."

I wandered back to my office shaking my head, sat at my desk and stared at my wall and the pictures of me in photo ops shaking hands with the politically famous.

Brenda answered on the second ring.

"I'm going into a meeting. What?"

"No one knows."

"What?"

"What happened Saturday night. Apparently, everyone but you was trashed. Group amnesia."

"You're not serious. This isn't one of your stupid jokes."

"What I'm telling you is real. I just talked to Ben. He doesn't know what happened the last hours of the party. Complete blank."

"I can't believe it."

"I'm having trouble myself, but it's true. Not only am I not going to get fired but I've just learned that there may be an opening for a promotion here. Wouldn't that be funny?"

"No... it wouldn't. Gotta go." She disconnected.

I reached into my desk drawer and pulled out personalized stationery so that I could write Ellie Redfern a handwritten "get-well-soon" note and thank her for the party.

II

Zoltan's Lie

After the first day of classes beginning the autumn semester, Zoltan and I resumed our practice of having a drink at the university club.

We sat at opposite ends of a small table in the bar, my beer and his vodka between us amongst small glass bowls of potato chips, pretzels and party mix.

Zoltan rummaged in the pretzel bowl, his colossal fingers almost unable to extract the loops.

We had just finished talking about our first impressions of this year's undergraduates who seemed ever younger and less prepared than the prior year's, inspiring in us headshaking disbelief.

There was an awkward pause, as often occurs when two colleagues resume meeting again after a long hiatus. Zoltan had spent much of the summer in his lab. I had spent mine shuttling our kids to various day camps and teaching a summer course. We were that close and had barely spoken to one another.

"So, what happened this summer on the home front?" I asked, wincing immediately at the inappropriate stupidity of the question.

Zoltan looked at me as if I had lost my mind. He spat out, "I have no home."

I watched members and guests at other tables look our way, eyeing him.

The fact is Zoltan frightens people.

More than his massive size and his hulking demeanor, it's the disturbed, crazy Hungarian seriousness of him that when he walks into a room causes people to shift uncomfortably, to glance about furtively for the closest exit. The unshaven mass of his scowling mustached countenance, penetrating black eyes, the coils of black-grey hair springing from his head—he looks as if he has emerged from some basement torture chamber for a breath of fresh air still absorbed in the work at hand. Zoltan moves through life unaware of the seas of humanity parting before him.

Putting all his idiosyncrasies aside, Zoltan is my good and loyal friend, the first person I would call in an emergency. I know many of his secrets; he knows way too many of mine.

For instance, we will have our drinks and Zoltan will pay me in cash for his portion as we exit the club. Despite being a tenured professor and senior cancer researcher, Zoltan is not a member of the club. He will pay me, an associate professor of communications, from the stash he keeps in his bottom bureau drawer -- his life savings.

Kicked out of his house by his wife years ago, living in a third-floor room he rents near the university, my friend is a man of the here and now. He and his wife fought over money for all their years of marriage and separation. He is on the one hand reluctant to get a divorce because of what it might cost him and on the other hand understandably paranoid about her knowing how much money he might actually have, so he has no bank account, no credit cards, no memberships. He pays his rent in person; he pays what few bills he might have by money order. I wonder at myself at times, because I have been immersed in Zoltan's life for so long, that all this seems normal to me.

"I'm sorry. I meant, how are things with your family?"

Zoltan made a dismissive wave of his hand, "Ack, the same. Ungrateful, spiteful—both Frida the shrew and Anna the college senior who think democracy suck."

"Maybe Anna will think different as time goes on."

"I don't know. As parent, I worry."

"All of us parents worry. That's the lead item in our job description."

"Yes, true. But you not seen, you not know what I know, what happened to Hungary in Second World War and after, what happen when not democracy. My Hungarian parents be turning over in their graves at what Anna think. So, I stay away from Anna. Just hand over money. It all bad. No good come of anything I do."

Then his whole countenance changes as he asks with real interest and concern, "How is Jan-net, and Sarah and Tommie?"

These inquiries are not only totally caring and sincere, but of an unusual depth and as such they routinely make me struggle to respond in some meaningful way. Unfortunately, no matter how I might try to embellish any description, our lives as two professionals raising two children in a metropolitan community are ones of frantic and mind-numbing routine.

I hear myself let out a small, exasperated sigh, "Janet? Good," I shrug, "Her practice is going well, but wearing her out. The usual."

"And Tommie and Sarah?"

"Good. Doing well in school."

Occasionally in emergencies we have had to call on Zoltan as a sitter for our kids. Uncle Zoltan. He invents experiments or games, totally ignores their bedtime, let's them eat sweets. By the time we return they are bouncing off the walls and in the midst of some odd scientific experiment, our kitchen turned into a rank smelling laboratory. Or he endeavors to teach them about his first love, opera, and we return home to opera blasting from the speakers and Zoltan acting out different parts with the kids, including female for which has borrowed some of Janet's clothes, which as you might imagine ticks her off pretty significantly. I mean, it's not like he can actually fit in any of her garments, so he pins them to himself. Needless to say, Tommie and Sarah find him endlessly amusing.

Our conversation lags for a moment.

Zoltan looks at me. "So, what is big problem?"

As usual, he has read my mind. I let out a sigh, take a long sip of beer. "Speaking of home. I can't go home tonight."

"So why you cannot go home?"

"Janet's college roommate is flying in today for a conference and spending tonight at our place."

"This is a problem?"

"Oh yeah."

"How this a problem?"

"Janet and I used to break-up regularly in college and in the first couple years out of college and on one of those occasions in our early 20's we were all in our first jobs and her college roommate, Lucy, was working in another city. Well, Janet and I broke up and somehow Lucy and I got it on for a weekend in a friend's house in Asheville, North Carolina. He wasn't there, of course. Managed to do it on every horizontal surface in that house and some not so horizontal. Total animals, ordered delivery and just kept at it hammer and tongs 24-7. Amazing weekend, but I haven't seen Lucy since, except at our wedding, where she shunned me. Just something not right about her and me long term, if you know what I mean. So, I just never followed up on our liaison."

"How she react to you doing that?"

"Oh, not well. Threatened to tell Janet and on and on. I'm amazed she never said anything but by then Janet and I had reconciled. That was our last big blow up and we got married the next spring.

"So, about a week ago I start getting emails from Lucy in advance of her visit. Friendly at first. She's looking forward to seeing me. Then they kinda slid into weirdness, like she's still hurt that I never followed up on our relationship. So, I'm thinking that if I go home at best there could be a very unpleasant scene, at worst, she's got some ricin in a baggie or maybe a nice carving knife in her purse or something."

"I like this crazy Lucy. I like this story. You in deep shit."

"Yeah," I said, shaking my head. "I am NOT going home. Gotta work late. Assemble all my lesson plans. May end up sleeping over in the office."

"You always do lesson plans in August because you asshole."

"You mean anal."

"Yes."

"You think Janet pays any attention to that? Maybe you should go home in my place."

"Yes, two women, one house. This good plan. But I have better plan. Uncle Zoltan to the rescue. I go home with you, be buffet."

"You mean, buffer."

"Yes."

While Zoltan was in the men's room, I called Janet to let her know he was joining us.

"Why would you do that?" she asked.

"Because he's a dear friend. He didn't have anywhere else to go this evening. And hell, Lucy's still single, right?"

"He's disreputable."

"Oh, I get it, for your dear friend we have to put on the best appearances."

"You know what I mean. I'm just glad you're coming home."

"What do you mean?"

"Oh, I thought maybe you'd find some excuse for not getting in until the crack of dawn."

"What makes you say that?"

"There's always some weird vibe that comes up whenever Lucy enters the conversation, like that maybe you don't like her for some reason."

"I don't know what you're talking about."

"You're a very poor liar, Thomas."

When Zoltan returned, I told him, "Everybody's excited you're coming to dinner, especially the kids."

"Wonderful."

"Man, I'm glad you're coming along. Janet just asked me why I don't like Lucy."

"Hmmm... Yes, your face give away everything all the time, Thomas."

"Shit."

We left the club as Zoltan shoved a wad of crumpled bills into my hand and walked across the quadrangle to my car in the crisp air, the setting sun illuminating the fall foliage amidst the general undergraduate celebration of cooler days, turning leaves, fraternity rush and an upcoming football game.

I drove out the expressway to our neighborhood, the neighborhood Janet and I thought would be so great and which we aren't wild about. It's pretty enough with relatively big, showy but cheaply built houses on small lots. What really attracted us was the great number of activities for the kids, the community pool, tennis courts and the nearby park and river. What we had not counted on were its very cliquey residents. The stay-at-home mommies hang out with their ilk as do the working mothers. Families who send their children to certain private schools hang out together. Families who go to the same church hang out together. On their own, the dads, immersed in their money-making pursuits, hang out with no one. Janet and I, whose life philosophies embrace independence, have discovered that we have little interest in hanging out with any of them. Often we feel like modern day seekers, looking for people of honesty and genuineness whose priorities are not skewed by false and ephemeral pursuits. It's a long and fruitless search. So, who the hell else would we invite over for dinner but Zoltan?

Twelve years is a long time and it was clear the moment I saw her that the years had not been unkind to Lucy. She still had the same raven hair, cut stylishly and professionally short now, fine pale skin, large light blue eyes, an expressive mouth that could be both tender and cynical.

But she was now a very different person than the girl I had partnered with on our wild weekend.

How would I have described the Lucy of the past? Well, the word libidinous comes to mind, aimless too, a fellow stoner.

Who did I now see standing in our hallway, holding a glass of chardonnay? An adult professional with a subtext of complex thoughts and emotions running through her expression. She was a bit bigger and broader, more woman there than before and she had a commanding presence now, confident, assertive.

Our eyes met and I could see and feel us both instantly flashback to our weekend together. Scenes, sounds, tastes, smells, sensations overwhelmed me and from what I could see, her. We stood for a moment in mutual paralysis.

Then her eyes shifted from mine to the doorway. I could see by the look on her face the impression Zoltan made coming in behind me, ducking and no doubt blocking out any view of the lawn and neighborhood.

At the same time, I glanced at Janet to gauge her reaction and frankly to take her in by way of comparison. My honey brown haired, brown eyed, no nonsense, practical to a fault, smart as a whip spouse who had more common sense than any crowd of people combined.

She had an amused and indulgent smile as she watched the proceedings. Good. I surmised that she and Lucy had no doubt been bonding over some wine and catch-up conversation for the last hour or so.

Tommie and Sarah rushed to Zoltan who went to one knee to accept their hugs.

"Can we play the *Nutcracker* again?" Tommie asked.

"Me too, me too," Sarah chimed in. "I am the best Sugar Plum Fairy!"

Lucy looked at them with mild surprise at the novelty of the situation while I could see Janet thinking defensively of how to protect her wardrobe.

"I cannot play tonight, children," he told them. "As difficult as it is, tonight I must play the much more tough role of grown up."

He stood and looked directly at Lucy.

"Zoltan at your service, madam." He bent carefully, took her hand and kissed it with his large moist lips.

I saw revulsion in Lucy's eyes but also a flash of ardor. Interesting, I thought.

"My," Lucy commented to Janet, "Isn't he charming." She turned to Zoltan. "Could I have my hand back, please. It's not a piece of barbecue."

"Yes, of course," Zoltan straightened and gave her back her hand.

"Well," I said helplessly, "Can I pour anyone some wine?"

"The kids have already eaten," Janet told us. "Let me get them upstairs and settled into their homework."

This is going to be awkward, I thought as we fetched glasses, cheese and crackers and the wine and went out to the family room.

As we settled in, Lucy turned to Zoltan and asked, "How did you develop an interest in opera?"

"It long story," he said, "I grow up outside Budapest. My father a physician there, want me to follow him in his practice but I have other idea. Always since I was little kid, I want to come to America. But I did take away one thing from my childhood. My parents' favorite thing in the world was the opera and we have a very good one in Budapest. We go as family whenever we can. I find as I grow up that I like it as much as they do. It is all life's drama wrapped into a performance. I think that American offer much more opportunity to succeed in the sciences, to be well paid and also much more freedom. So, I apply and win a scholarship to study in America for a year in New York. I get to America and my professors like me and I persuade them to offer me a job in the laboratory and eventually as I work and study, I apply for citizenship. I even take my professors to the opera and they become interested and we form a group of science people who like the arts. I pay for my parents to visit often while they alive and we spend a lot of time traveling to different cities to see different operas and theatres and then I travel back to Europe and we go to the best theatres there. Parents both gone now but my fascination with opera continue. So, you here for conference, tell me about that?"

"I'm a director of an animal shelter so am involved in a national animal protection organization and this year the conference is here, so I thought it would be a good time to catch up with old friends."

"So, you and Thomas and Janet were wild and crazy kids in college."

"Well," said Lucy, looking at me, "Yes, we were on occasion, even after college."

"Ah, that good."

For the next half hour we force-talked the usual drivel – weather, Lucy's flight in from O'Hare, where her conference was being held, how our area had grown, the impossible traffic. While we made conversation, I found my mind drifting onto the subject of Janet and myself and our compatibility and comfort with one another versus the misfit of Lucy and I and why things were like that with one person who became your mate and with the other who would never.

Janet returned and sat down with her glass of wine which she had retrieved from the kitchen.

"So, how was your day?" I asked.

"Oh, I saw my favorite client today."

"Opps, sorry, I didn't know that. He'll make it another week?"

She shrugged. "One can't be sure. Anti-depressants can only do so much. He's very determined and willful to be forever unhappy, so it's a struggle to keep him upright."

After a time, we moved through the kitchen into the dining room, all of us bringing out the dinner of meat loaf, scalloped potatoes and green beans that had been warming in the oven, an instant meal for a harried family.

We talked some more about the kids, their schools and what we liked and disliked about them, filling Lucy in on the neighborhood and the area.

Zoltan asked, "So, Lucy, what is it that you do with this animal shelter?"

"Well, actually I've just accepted a new job to head the largest animal shelter in Illinois, just outside of Chicago."

"That is very good and interesting. How did you come to do that?"

"Well, after college I hit a bit of a rough spot with a lover who abandoned me," Lucy said.

Zoltan gave me a quick glance as he put a fork full of scalloped potatoes into his mouth.

"So, I quit my job and moved back to my parent's house outside of Chicago and with nothing much to do except feel sorry for myself, I volunteered at a local humane society. Liked it. There's a whole lot more empathy available from animals it seems than human beings. They had an opening for an assistant. Well, that worked for me. And here I am twelve years later with this new appointment," she shrugged, smiling, obviously pleased with herself.

Lucy turned to Janet and me, "So, how are you guys?"

I was sure that she and Janet had covered this territory prior to Zoltan and my arrival, so I intuited this was actually a direct question for me.

"Oh, happily stuck in a rut," I said as sincerely as possible, hoping that this would be both reasonably and boringly truthful. Then to deflect her attention, I said, "I can see you've changed a good deal though. We all do I guess."

"Oh, I don't know," said Janet, looking at me, "I think some of us go along and just become more and more caricatures of ourselves."

I lifted my glass immediately in a toast. "To caricatures!" I was thinking Jee-sus.

Janet lifted her glass, an expression on her face that she was having a bit of fun with me but clueless as to what expense, and Zoltan and Lucy joined us.

"So, Zoltan," Lucy asked, "what do you do?"

"Well, I professor teaching medical students and I am involved in a good deal of research."

"Oh. What kind of research?"

"I am the one doing everything no one wants to hear about. It involves canines mostly."

"Really."

I looked at Zoltan quizzically. He rarely talked about his cancer research at the club and never in our company at home, so I knew immediately what he had just said was a complete fabrication, a fact that Janet would not pick up. Where the hell was he going with this?

Zoltan continued, "Yes, it is heavily supported by the tobacco industry and their associations. I teach the dogs how to smoke and then I dissect them to discover any harm that may be caused. Then I write up a report providing, what is the word that has been used? Oh, yes, 'due-bious' findings and submit them."

Lucy's face blanched, "You kill dogs for a living?"

"Hey, somebody got to do it."

"How is it that you never told us this before?" Janet asked incredulous.

Zoltan shrugged, "You never ask."

Lucy's knife and fork clattered onto her plate.

She stood, and we watched in fascination as her chalky complexion of shock gave way to a mottled crimson of fury.

She turned to Janet.

"This is your *friend*?"

Shocked and horrified, Janet looked at her and was speechless.

"I'm sorry," Lucy said, "I cannot abide this monster being here. I'm leaving. I'll stay at the conference hotel tonight or somewhere nearby."

She turned to Zoltan, "What you do is criminal!" she shouted at him.

Zoltan sat there with an inexplicably neutral, almost innocent, expression that conveyed no contrition whatsoever.

Lucy stormed through the kitchen and hallway,

pounded up the stairs to collect her suitcase, pounded back down the stairs and slammed the front door behind her.

Janet turned on Zoltan.

"I don't know that you are welcome in this house anymore."

"But Jan-net, you must."

"Give me one good reason why?"

"I make it all up. It a big joke. I just teach courses and am cancer researcher. Don't do any of that research I just talk about. That research done by others. I only know about it; I don't do it."

"It was not *one bit* funny, Zoltan," she replied angrily.

He bowed his head, "Yes, I realize that now. I am sorry."

Zoltan gave me a glance with the briefest hint of a smile flashing across his features. Well, he had certainly solved any problem I might have with Lucy. But damn.

"You drove off my best friend," Janet exclaimed. "How could you do that?"

"Do not worry. I see her in the morning. Take her to breakfast. Everything be okay."

"How so?" Janet asked snidely.

"I will explain that I am very bad joker and liar and beg her forgiveness."

"And you think that will work?" Janet asked. "How will you get in touch with her?"

"You have her cell number, yes?"

"Well... yes."

"I text her big apology, then call."

Janet and I looked at one another for a long moment, looked back at Zoltan. I found myself shaking my head slowly in exact time with Janet.

"I hope you know what the hell you are doing," I told him.

Friday and the weekend went by without a word from Lucy or Zoltan, which seemed very odd. But while we were dying of curiosity, neither of us could bring ourselves to call either one. Finally, I texted Zoltan, suggesting we get together for a drink after work on Monday.

He arrived fresh shaven with a haircut and a spring in his step.

"You look chipper," I told him.

"Yes, I am getting in shape. I start now walking every morning, but it strange. I walk in the neighborhood and people, when they see me, they walk across the street and then walk down the opposite sidewalk. Why is that?"

"Beats me," I shrugged. "So, what the hell happened with Lucy?"

"Oh, I text her a very sincere and humble apology and call her the next morning at her hotel. I surprised she answer call, but she did. After some being not too certain she agreed to have coffee with me at the conference hotel, so I shower, I shave, I take cab and meet her there. I bring a gift and I explain I am a big fool who does not know how to be funny."

"And she bought that?"

"I am charming, yes?"

"What was the gift?"

"A contribution for her new shelter."

"That's pretty clever. How much?"

"Ten thousand dollars."

"Very charming."

"Yes, it very funny too because in restaurant I give her all these $100 bills from bottom drawer. I worry it look like drug deal. So, I had thought of this and I put money in a nice gift bag I buy at drug store and enclose a note I write saying that I am so pleased to give this gift to her shelter."

"So, she liked the gift, I take it."

"Yes, a lot. Instead of going to her conference, I take her to see my lab, talk to her about what we doing trying to cure cancer through immunology. She seem very impressed, so then we had our own conference."

"Ahhh..."

"Thomas, how did you ever give that up? I do not know whether to think less of you or more of you or a great deal more of Janet."

"Let's leave it that with Janet things are very different as well as being very good."

"So, now I need your help."

"You need *my* help?

"Yes. I must buy new clothes. Things like you wear. I am going to Chicago for this weekend."

"Whoa. Very good. Sure, I'll help."

"Then Lucy coming here next weekend. We date double."

"Fantastic. Janet will be thrilled."

"And we getting you present."

"Ummmn... Hell, I don't want to ask.... What?"

"We adopt you a dog. We date double. Go to shelter."

"Zoltan, that's the last thing we need right now."

"Lucy and I agree, you both uptight suburban pinch faces."

"Come on. Cut the crap."

"It true. You both need something new and different.

Plus the kids want a dog very bad. They say you both crap all over them about this."

"Yeah, but that's our issue, not something for you guys to interfere with."

"I uncle."

"In a manner of speaking."

"Lucy and I help you and Janet pick out dog next weekend."

I sighed, looking at my friend. "Janet's right," I told him, "You are disreputable."

III

Gohn

F ace it. He intimidates people. While this sometimes served him well as the chairman and CEO of
Piper-Hale, a conglomerate he founded some fif-
ty-plus years ago, it is not at all a winning attribute for his
new role as president of the Gaylord and Helen McDonald
Family Foundation where empathy, listening and learning should be at the forefront of what we do. So, it is now
left to me, as the foundation's first executive director, to
curb this tendency and bend it toward the sweetness and
light befitting his new role.

A big challenge. In part because he is a big man, 6'6" tall,
long limbed and wide shouldered. He played center for his
Ivy basketball team many decades ago and was known for
his sweeping hook shot where, while the ball rolled gracefully off his fingers toward the basket, his unnoticed out-
flung left arm not so gracefully clobbered his defender. He
still carries himself with the confidence inspired by those
times, with a subconscious tendency to sweep past people,
leaving them feeling dismissed or ignored.

Then, as he has aged, there is his bird of prey visage,
his large, hooked nose, combed back white hair, gnarled
tufts of white eyebrows, speckled frame glasses, disap-
proving mouth, prominent chin, piercing blue eyes.

This is not to say that if it is in his interest he cannot quickly transform and become utterly charming. Nevertheless, he is not an easy man to get to know or with whom to establish trust.

Now that we were on the phone going over the last-minute details for our first site visit, I brought up what had been nagging me all week but which, not wanting to come across as confrontational, I had not mentioned until now.

"So, Dad, please, could you not dress corporate? Instead, wear something casual but respectful. You have a tendency to cause people to clam up, you know. We're there to have these folks tell us about their mission, accomplishments and needs. Okay?"

"Whatever you say, Alicia," he said in a tone that told me he was only mildly pissed-off by my advice. I breathed a sigh of relief.

"You've read the briefing materials I sent? The Gohn Food and Outreach Center?"

"Of course, my dear. Frankly, I was stunned by the size of the problem of hunger here, not to mention nationally, and by the size and diversity of service this organization and their partnerships provide. What they are doing is remarkable – over 600 partner agencies from food companies and grocery chains to various social service organizations, schools and community organizations, feeding over 250,000 people a year, all their related educational programs aimed at uplifting and stabilizing, making recipients ready for employment, including a career track program training folks for the food service industry, programs for families in need, the elderly, even pre-school families. Quite impressive. I can see why you've chosen them for our first visit. Looking forward to it."

"Fabulous. You're making me proud." I was delighted by the depth of his interest.

"But, my dear, there are some worrisome aspects about their operations, particularly budgetarily. Between their annual report and their 990 tax return, nothing adds up or syncs."

"The annual report for a non-profit is often a PR/marketing piece that puts them in the best light possible."

"Hmmm..."

"Dad this isn't a multi-billion-dollar corporation we're calling on. As you can see, their entire budget is only $9+ million."

"If we make a grant to them, it's an investment, don't you think?"

"Ok..."

"Just like any investor large or small we have the right to know what our likely return on investment is. Financial reports need to be transparent."

"Theoretically, yes, but most non-profits don't run that way. They're focused on mission delivery not so much accounting. Think small staff, rudimentary systems."

"If you say so, but I'm also troubled by this bifurcated governance system of theirs."

"Yeah, actually I am too. They have a board of directors which operates like a normal board, have committees for finance, fundraising, public relations, special events, board development etc. Then there are references made in places to a corporate board. Difficult to know exactly what that is. Let's ask about it."

"And they've been expanding, placing new distribution centers in three sites across the city. Where's the capital budget and the accounting for that?"

I sighed. "Nowhere to be found."

"I smell debt and possibly cover-up at the corporate board level."

"God damn it, Dad. Lighten up!"

"I will try oh so hard, honey." I could see his cynical smile. "See you there." The bird of prey had spoken.

For years I had avoided any business involvement with my father and no wonder. Growing up my parents seemed to think I was one of their possessions. You know, trot out little Alicia to show off some aspect of my upbringing that would impress their friends. That only lasted so long and when I ceased cooperating, they sent me to boarding school. Somehow I not only survived but prospered, no doubt because I seem to have inherited a very strong desire to succeed, probably from the old man.

After boarding school, I went to Georgetown. That my father was on the board of regents might have had something to do with my acceptance, but I chose to believe otherwise. The fact was that Georgetown presented the best diversity of programs in which I was interested.

Gradually at Georgetown I seem to have worked through most of my daddy issues, became my own person I am proud to say, majored in political science and then received a law degree there.

Of course, upon my graduation from law school my father wanted me to join Piper-Hale but I had other ideas. Talk about pursuing the path less traveled, I shunned Piper-Hale and the big, smug law firms and became a private detective, working for The Blaylock Agency in DC, one of the larger agencies of its kind in the world.

This career move made for hilarious event conversations at Piper-Hale, Georgetown alumni and other professional cocktail parties or events when asked what I did for a living and I replied that I was a private investigator. My fellow conversationalist, his or her eyes would flash a momentary "Ohhh, shit!" recognition before shifting to the usual insincere interest, eyes wandering around the room for an immediate escape. In a few cases with an expression of absolute shock, despair and panic, my "colleague" would turn on his or her heel and head for the door. One could almost smell burning rubber.

Despite being utterly socially and politically incorrect, it was this erstwhile career decision and vocation that taught me to be self-reliant, gave me numerous useful skills from picking locks to hacking into hard drives and allowed me to see slices of lives gone wrong that were educational way beyond the classroom, life lessons in every case we had.

I saw my parents infrequently. Each time I visited them, I was struck by their aging and how my father's attitude toward me was changing. Instead of being the imperious dictator, he began to be far more collegial. Instead of my mother and I fighting his schedule to find a time to be together as a family, it was he who was offering ideas about togetherness. Every so often he would suggest that he and I attend some event together. Occasionally, he would seek my perspective about a legal matter. Once he sought my advice about a situation where an officer of the company was suspected of compromising himself. Could The Blaylock Agency verify the problem behind the scenes without anyone being the wiser? It turned out that we could, *gratis*, which scored points and, I thought, helped establish us as colleagues.

Then a year ago, after Christmas, when I was home, he invited me to his office for a "chat".

I went out and bought a serious power suit and on the day of our appointment rode with my father in the company limousine downtown to Piper-Hale.

There we went through all the security and took the elevator, which goes up very rapidly and forever to the point where there's this wave effect of noise which is actually from the building moving in the wind as the elevator goes straight up. Your ears pop along the way. And, finally, we reach the executive offices and his suite.

He very kindly introduced me around and then we went into his office and he closed the door and we sat at a nice little hospitality area by a floor-to-ceiling window looking out over the city to infinity, and he told me how proud he was of me and asked me about how things were going at Blaylock, whether I had a boyfriend or significant other, to which I replied no, not really, and he was interested in what plans I might have for the future.

I told him that I was completely undecided, a lot of different options, but I was not of a mind to pursue any of them at the moment, just biding my time.

My news, I could see, was encouraging to my father. He gave some thought to what I had just said, taking a long, cogitating look at the cityscape beyond the window, and then he turned to me. I got a sense, perhaps the first time I had seen this in him, that he was anxious. I could see how much he cared about what he was about to say to me. That was a shock that he cared so much. What was at stake, I realized, was his relationship with me, and that he would be crushed if he lost it, even though he had been distant to me most of my life. I realized this was not about his being a big, powerful CEO but about me being his daughter and him being my father. Kind of blew my mind.

My father said, "I have a position to fill that I would like you to consider."

As it turned out, he was getting ready to step away from the company he founded. Part of this was his decision, part of it was with the encouragement of the board of directors. So, step one of his exit plan was appointing a CEO and holding only the title of chairman, and then shortly thereafter, becoming chairman emeritus and in essence retiring. Well, retiring as much as anyone like him can retire. While he was ceding day-to-day management responsibility, he would still be involved.

Of course, he is keeping his preferred shares which allow him a significant voting say in how the company moves forward.

But the interesting part was that over the next year he would be transferring a significant portion of his common shares and stock options over to a family foundation.

The new role he saw for himself was to become a major philanthropist and for me to be his partner in that endeavor.

We had a long discussion about all the good that the foundation could accomplish funding sustainability, new technologies, private and public sector initiatives, the environment, for education and training for the disadvantaged.

I thought about his offer for several days and, finally,

accepted. It was time to move back to my hometown, buy my own place, a nice condo near downtown, establish an office for the foundation and get to work.

The Gohn Food and Outreach Center is headquartered in a massive, nondescript two story facility attached to its central warehouse in an industrial park at the northeast end of town, not a place to be driven to directly if you value your life, and an awkward place to reach via several highways. I was early for our 8:00am appointment on a crisp spring day and sat in my car for about ten minutes near the front of their office and warehouse watching a beehive of activity as semi-trucks from grocery chains and food manufacturers unloaded at loading docks and food delivery trucks left the garage. As well, individuals and families arrived via shuttle buses, derelict cars and vans, by bike and on foot and entered the building.

In setting up this meeting I had talked numerous times with the agency's executive director, a Ms. Maureen Brooke. Ms. Brooke was a bit formal, on the edge of being baleful and it was difficult for me to know how to interpret her reserved manner. Hiding something? Not thrilled to be visited by rich, white people? Or perhaps she simply enjoyed being borderline difficult with anyone she viewed as beneath her. You would think that my last name being McDonald might contain a subtle hint of someone not to trifle with. But I just let it go out of my interest in seeing how her attitude would play out at our meeting, especially to see her reaction to my father and his reaction to her.

We would be joined by Gilbert Gohn, the naming founder of the agency and chair of their corporate board.

At 8:00am exactly, Ms. Brooke, a large woman with a broad, commanding face and permed hair, in a too tight purple floral print on white background dress, stepped out of the front door of the agency and scanned the area. I promptly exited my car and waved to her. She acknowledged me with a nod of her head and as I walked toward her a cab pulled up and my father extricated himself from it. I was so pleased to see him dressed in casual clothes, blue serge slacks, a tan zip jacket and a light blue dress shirt, walking shoes. He had even ditched his platinum Rolex for a sports watch.

With my father on the scene the redoubtable Ms. Brook's countenance made a dramatic change. Suddenly she was delighted to see both of us.

"Welcome," she greeted us as we shook hands. "We're so honored to have you visit our agency, Mr. and Ms. McDonald. Let me give you a brief tour and then we'll meet with our chair, Mr. Gilbert Gohn."

"The mission of our agency," she told us as we entered the building, "Is not simply helping to eliminate hunger but, using our programs to combat hunger as a first step to motivate our clients to help improve their lives. In many cases, they didn't wish their circumstances on themselves, they just fell into a spiral of bad judgements and/or circumstances that left them without any resources. Our outreach and counseling programs work with our clients in all walks of life and circumstances to try to help them break their cycle of poverty and lost opportunity through counseling them on resources available. As well, we provide employment counseling and training. Our mission is one of hope and motivation not maintenance."

We walked hallways of built out classrooms and offices, the classrooms well populated and each office addressing the needs of clients, all of them, as Ms. Brooke explained, going about the business of outreach and redemption – family counseling, employment counseling, benefits advice, programs for seniors, for families with pre-school children, medical services, psychological services. Ms. Brooke outlined how each program related step-by-step to the participants' ability to access further programs. As she continued, I noticed how her manner became much more comfortable, facts and figures at hand, a sage ability to show us how each program fit into and related to the organization's mission. This was her agency and she was proud of it and fully invested in it. I began to understand her reserved manner. Outsiders could not possibly fully grasp the enormous and complicated accomplishment of the agency, which ran like a well-oiled machine. I was glad I had cut her some slack.

We ended by touring the food hall, adjacent to the market, where an array of people seemingly of all ages and from all walks of life were having breakfast.

As we passed through the food hall, my father stopped abruptly, stared intently out into the back corner of the hall, his expression at first questioning, then recognition, then I thought I saw a flicker of sadness before he changed his expression back to normalcy.

I found Ms. Brooke looking at him with concern, as if she suspected him of having an incipient stroke.

"Um, what's of interest?" I asked him.

"Ah, I beg your pardon," he said to both of us. "I was

just noting that many of your clients seem to know one another and are enjoy one another's company."

"Quite true," Ms. Brooke replied, "We manage in many cases to build some esprit de corps. Thank you for noticing."

"That's a wonderful accomplishment. Somehow I had expected something quite different." He shrugged. "I thought I would see despondency. Instead, I see hope. Quite inspiring."

We took an elevator to the second floor while I puzzled over my father's lapse. Something had occurred in the Food Hall that I was clueless about.

Walking down a long, poorly lit, industrial hallway, we came to an ornate mahogany door and entered into an expansive board room, its décor quite august, mahogany paneled walls, an outsized mahogany board room table surrounded by leather bound, faux Chippendale chairs on castors, all on a remarkable, plush oriental rug, lighting provided by Tiffany lamps.

Gohn was sitting at the end of the table as if presiding over a meeting. In the corner sat a man of medium height, close cut grey hair, a broad muscular build, dressed in black, black shirt, black tie, black suit, black crepe soled shoes, his hands and the way he held himself communicating an ability to destroy with a few quick motions. He watched us with guarded and almost insolent expression but made no move to greet us. Gohn rose, a small man of bent stature, "Welcome!" he half shouted with a hollow voice, in the manner of those who are hard of hearing, making a grandiose gesture as if he were welcoming the universe.

We walked to him and shook his dead carp hand, Ms. Brooke standing respectfully to the side.

"You may wondah about this grand décor of our board room," Gohn said proudly.

"Yes," my father said, "As impressive as it is out of place."

"Hah! That's what everybody says or that's what they think anyway. Well, on this here board room, you'll appreciate, Mr. McDonald, that the price was right."

"Was it?"

"As in free."

"My, my, the best price of all."

"Yeah. We was demolishin' the old Mercantile bank buildin' downtown. You know I grew up in bizness with that god damned bank. You musta too. Bunch of green eyeshades over there then. Couldn't get no good terms on anything. You know what they called the place, I guess."

"Yes," my father smiled.

"Jerkcantile!" Gohn erupted with a contemptuous snort of a laugh glancing around at each one of us to be sure his remark was fully appreciated. "Anyhow, we was demonlishin' the place, which gave me great satisfaction, and came across this gem. I said, hell it's too f...ing nice to demolish, so I had my guys very carefully dismantle it and move it here. So, no delusions of grandeur, just a lucky find on my part. I love bein' here and using their stuff to make my own decisions about finance and funding. Kinda feel like I'm gettin' even."

"Quite understandable," my father remarked, "Well done." I could see the charm kicking in as he played to Gohn's big as all outdoors ego.

I had done extensive background research on Gilbert

Gohn, a man who had made a fortune in real estate investment, buying his first apartment building over a half a century ago and parlaying it through a succession of positive cash flow purchases into a massive portfolio of apartment buildings, garages, commercial and residential real estate and real estate services, construction and new neighborhood development. He began, it appeared, as a slum lord, gradually building a more diversified and respectable empire during which time he began evermore magnanimous, the Food and Outreach Center becoming his primary philanthropic focus.

"Let me introduce you to Mr. Arkin, my driver and valet. My dear wife passed two years ago and it's not a great idea for me to be livin' alone. Mr. Arkin keeps me safe. She was one tough woman, iddn't that true?" he asked Arkin.

"Tough." Arkin said in a voice the somehow contained an impossible mixture of dry ice and sand.

"But not tough enough to beat luke-kemia. John Hopkins couldn't save her like they saved me with prostrate. I gave 'em a chair anyway. Have a seat," Gohn encouraged. "Have a seat."

My father and I sat to his left. Ms. Brooke walked behind him and sat on his right. I began to think that Mr. Gohn and his driver/valet might also have something to do with her reserved manner. Not exactly the image you would want to share with the rest of the world.

"So, whaddaya think of your tour?" Gohn asked us.

"Quite impressive," my father told him. "I'm frankly amazed at the size and scope of this agency's accomplishment, its well thought out, interrelated programs and perhaps most surprising to me, the esprit de corps."

"Well, my friend, you can thank Ms. Brooke for all that.

Let me tell you about this marvelous lady," he told us in what I sensed were well rehearsed lines, "who in my opinion is qualified for sainthood. Without her this agency would be nothin'. She makes it all work. I'm pleased to see finally, now that I got some flacks in my bizness to get her some press, she and the center are getting some of the public recognition she deserves. 'Bout time. Anyway, she's a godsend to this agency."

At this praise, Ms. Brooke looked down at her hands, folded on her lap.

Feeling that I should help direct the conversation, I asked, "Tell us about your current and future needs. How could our foundation help further your mission? What impact would our gift make? How do you measure such impact?"

"Our biggest need," Ms. Brooke told us, "Is with our counseling, job training and related services to break the spiral of failure and desperation our clients often find themselves in. You noticed the vehicles that pulled up this morning. Many of the folks having breakfast with us today are living in those vehicles. I'd be happy to send you a proposal on behalf of such programs and the impact they have on our clients' ability to find employment - how many of our clients your funding would enable to chart a new life."

"That would be excellent," I commented.

My father said to Gohn, "Let me ask you about this corporate board of yours. Exactly how is it structured? How does it interface with the organization?"

"Ah," Gohn said, "I knew you'd be askin' me that. You're a smart man, Mr. McDonald. The fact is it's a corporate board in name only. I jus' decided one day to call it that. It's my baby, has no governance nor any other kinda relationship to the center. That's the way I like it. No red tape. No small minded pissants interferein' with my bizness. What the corporate board is is my giving to the center, me and my biznesses, holding companies ex cetera. I use it as a conduit for my philanthropy to the center for projects that are too important, complicating and distracting for them to undertake. For instance, the center is expanding its food outreach services to different parts of the city where they are badly needed. I'm financing this endeavor, more than a couple million bucks, with my philanthropy. The buildin' projects are being undertaken at cost, no mark-up, by my development companies or other companies and subcontractors who owe me favors. They're doing it as a sideline, but a priority sideline, to their regulah business."

We talked another twenty minutes or more about the specifics of their proposal. They sought guidance about the amount of their request and my father said that was something we would need to confer about and that I would get back to them.

We all stood finally and Gohn walked with us to the board room door, thanking us for coming. Ms. Brooke guided us to the elevator and the front door. We shook hands and expressed to one another our appreciation for the visit.

We turned and walked away.

"Could I prevail upon you to give me a ride home?" my father asked.

"Sure."

On the way, my father turned to me and said, "Well, my dear, that was a most interesting visit. I'm looking forward to more adventures of this type."

"Yeah, same here. But what the hell happened there in the food hall?"

"Ah, in the depths of the room I recognized a Mr. Boyce Hale. Name sound familiar?"

"Well, yes, of course."

"My college classmate, alcoholic, who owned with his partner, the clothing goods manufacturer I bought out more than and half century ago and used as the platform to build what today is Piper-Hale, same name, now a conglomerate. Mr. Hale was delusional in his thinking about his original company. Utterly defeated when he had to sell. Never got over it really. And today, there he was, his station in life where I might have expected it to be. Quite disturbing and sad."

"I can only imagine."

"We create our own destiny, my dear, as I'm sure you must realize. So many in life think they are the victim of external forces. The world is against them. In fact, it is they who are against themselves."

We paused for a moment, reflecting.

"What do you think is going on there with Mr. Gohn and his corporate board?" I asked.

My father smiled, shrugged, "We'll never know and the fact is, we do not want to know. At the very least he has a very interesting tax deduction shell game going on. Not impossible that not all the money he's providing to the agency through his corporate board is his own."

"You mean, he could be laundering money. The thought occurred to me."

"Exactly. In any case, if one were to investigate the ownership of the contractors and subs being employed to build the new centers, a somewhat accurate picture might emerge of the *modus operandi*."

"You want me to research that?"

"No, not at all. Whatever the ill-gotten nature of this, its outcome is benefitting the citizens of this city. Its disruption for any reason would further imperil many of them living on the edge, like my god forsaken classmate. No, no... Let's turn our heads in the other direction. I think we should give them some guidance on submitting a proposal for, say, $300,000, on behalf of their counseling and education programs. That's the best we can do for them, their clients and for our foundation. Oh, and let's anonymously, through Ms. Brooke, find a way to provide a gift of, say, $10,000 to Boyce Hale. If it can be masqueraded in some way as a grant, award or even better a monthly stipend of some sort, so much the better."

"Ok, whatever you say. I'm sure Ms. Brooke will be delighted."

"I'm sure she will. As for Mr. Gohn," he paused and smiled, "I couldn't care less."

"Well, his heart's in the right place."

"If by that you mean his anus, yes, quite correct."

"Dad!"

He turned and smiled at me. The bird of prey had spoken.

IV

Neophyte

| ADAPTED FROM *From the Midst of Wickedness* |

I had wondered how the other half lived. Now I was finding out.

The weather had been twenty-seven degrees and sleeting when I had left Janet's and my warm bed this morning, showered and dressed quietly to be sure not to wake her or the kids and driven in the dark to the airport.

At Miami International a small Cuban driver in a Guayabera, holding up a handwritten sign with my name, Thomas Simpson, scrawled on it, met me at the airport passenger exit. We made our way to a limousine which had a bar, newspapers, magazines and internet. The driver sped along a series of highways, finally exiting onto a rural road and then turning into the long driveway of a pristine resort, passing lakes filled with exotic birds and bordered by an array of palm trees and flowering plants.

After checking into the Calypso Too Hotel, where the university's board meeting was being held the next day, I followed the bellboy to a metal cage elevator which took us to the third floor. We made our way down a clean white stucco and tile hallway to my room at the end. Inside, its sliding doors opened to a balcony overlooking the ocean.

I freshened up and changed into summer slacks, a short sleeve shirt and a blazer, then stood on the balcony for a time to take in the ocean, the sound of the surf, the beauty of the shoreline and beach.

The board's cocktail reception was just beginning when I stepped out on the terrace opposite the hotel's entrance. A cool breeze was blowing in from the ocean as the sun began to set. A waiter approached me and took my order for a beer.

Wentz, a crony of the president and the dean of the College of Continuing Education, Frank Lusby, our capital campaign consultant and Bernie Reve, the director of advancement were standing off to the left.

I walked over to them, "How're you guys?"

Wentz motioned at me with his usual martini in his fat hand, "So, Thomas, you smell anything?"

"You're not that close, thankfully."

"Ah," Reve commented, smiling, "Good. I love it when people insult Wentz.... It seems so... right."

"Thomas," Wentz observed, ignoring both of our comments, "I smell the sweetest scent of all."

Reve and Lusby looked at one another knowingly.

"What would that be?"

"Money! Money, money, money. Take a deep inhale, Thomas. It's all around you."

I looked around. "Really?"

"The net worth of the individuals on this terrace is greater that the GDP of Nicaragua, not to mention the hundred plus other countries ranked below it."

"Jesus." I looked around at the board members gathered there.

"Hey, Bernie," Lusby said to Reve, "Give our friend a tour of the board members, will you? He needs to know who they are."

"Yeah, sure. Let me introduce you to our greatest champions at least by profile," Reve said, reaching out, taking my arm and guiding me to the corner of the terrace to be sure his lesson would be unobserved. He motioned to the different people on the terrace with his Manhattan.

"There's Fritz Johnson, the board chair, obviously a Texan, not an oilman, a lawyer. They say the lawyers end up with all the money and in the boom and bust of Texas it seems that he has ended up with a good bit of it. Shrewd mother fucker, Washington ambitious which makes him and our president soul mates of a sort. Around here we call him "Big Johnson" not only because of his size but because clearly he's also got a big one litigation wise. Runs a tight board meeting, doesn't suffer fools gladly."

"Well, I'm fucked then."

Reve looked at me evenly. "I wouldn't say that. The president thinks that your branding us as The Global University and with the marketing and communications plans you've laid out for the future that you're the goose who's going to lay him a world class golden egg."

"No pressure, huh?"

"You said it, not me. Maggie Garnet, there, hovering in the president's aura, is an alumna, former bank CEO, now head of the Federal Reserve in Kansas City. Frank, her husband who is not here owns Garnetvision Communications. You've undoubtedly read about them given all the consolidation going on in that industry and the FTC and FCC getting bent out of shape by it.

"Tyson Wiggins, over there, might look like a geeky black kid but he founded three successful tech companies before he was 26. Now in VC in the Silicon Valley.

"Mark Berger, there, by the dais is our great host. Owns this place, as you may know. Billionaire hedge fund owner. Has given the university some incredibly good investment advice. Keeps his distance. Throws an occasional 50k at us here and there. Can't get to know him well enough to know his interests."

Reve nodded. "Morris Ortiz, there, founded Ortiz Capital, a conglomeration of mutual funds. You've undoubtedly seen their ads in Fortune, Forbes, WSJ. He and Berger get into polite and not so polite disputes on investment policy on occasion. Fascinating stuff. God, these guys are sharp. Way over my head.

"Tunstall (Tunny) S. Slingluff V, there, local boy made good, media empire he inherited from his family. Selling it off piece by piece because that's about the only way to go these days. Interesting how fortunes ebb, like with the Slingluffs, and flow, like with the Garnets.

"Beatrice Fontaine, there. Ms. Fontaine. New York City. Billionairess. Inheritance. Likes her men socially prominent, slim and mean and her martinis dry. Divorced three times. Now I think she just hangs around with the gardener. Saves money.

"Allan Gunderson, there, former owner of a bond trading company. Total wild man, funniest and most creative thinker in this room but watch him. Just when you least expect it, he'll grab your ass, my ass, particularly, Ursula, the president's assistant's ass. There is no stopping him, especially as the evening and the drinks go on. He thinks that's funny. He's the only one.

"Over there Senator Egon Maxwell looks the part doesn't he with the swept back mane and those big eyebrows? A complete cypher. Say whatever you want. He'll agree with you. He is very helpful with our federal relations, however. Very crafty in regard to our sponsored research grants.

"Jonathan Melfur, talking with the president, is the board president of the Melfur Foundation, grandson of the founder, chairman and CEO of Melfur Inc., the insurance conglomerate that ol' grandad started in his great grandparents' attic bedroom.

"Oh, and there's the honorable provost, Dr. Kravitz, talking with Ms. Fontaine. Not a board member but here to report on things academic. What a prick. The provost, I mean. Ms. Fontaine may have one for all I know or something down there with teeth."

I looked at Kravitz and saw that he was working hard, so hard that his natural charm had turned unctuous, his head bobbing and his hands moving as if being worked by an invisible puppeteer for an act that was all about ulterior motives. Clearly Ms. Fontaine was not suffering him gladly as she smiled a saccharine smile and glanced around the room for other company.

I wondered what was driving him. Self-importance, certainly. Jealousy, it was well known that he felt the university's presidency should have gone to him, not Bryan Q. Fitz-Hugh, our present visionary charmer. Moral outrage at the continuing emphasis of the university on a curriculum stressing post college employment over the time immemorial virtues of the humanities? Justified? Hard to know. His whole presence gave me an uneasy feeling.

Bernie continued, "We have a couple presidents and

CEOs. See those two gentlemen over there talking with one another? The one on the left is the chairman of Oxyidite Pharmaceuticals. The guy he's talking with is the president of Allogenic Technology. Both of them and their wives are absolutely charming, intelligent, well-read, cultured, love you so long as you have some business or social value to them. Otherwise you're dirt. Personally, while they all think I'm wonderful for the prestige and connections and just plain suck I can bring to them at the university, I find them to be cyborgs with Machiavellian programming. Hearts of stone or maybe titanium. Cold mechanical mother fuckers."

"Wow, Bernie, that's pretty harsh."

"Yeah? Is it? I don't think so."

"Okay."

He downed the remainder of his Manhattan. "Well, let's get the hell to dinner. I feel a sudden spasm of charm coming on."

We walked from the terrace back into and through the hotel to another terrace on the south side overlooking the ocean where a tent had been installed under tall palms. Linen tablecloths graced tables set with heavy silverware, crystal wine glasses for white and red, centerpieces of orchids, hibiscus, bougainvillea, bird of paradise, place cards at each setting. The sun cast an orange light over the ocean and beach below us, the surf sounding a gentle rhythm to our gathering. Lights on poles came on as I began looking at each table for the place card with my name on it.

I found my seat and glanced at the first course salad of fresh grilled mahi glazed with a macadamia and orange dressing on a bed of small spinach leaves and stood by my chair while the others walked in.

Looking at the place cards on either side I saw that Ursula had placed me between Allan Gunderson and Ms. Fontaine.

Gunderson arrived, bourbon on the rocks in hand, flush-faced and in a jovial mood.

"Good evening!" he greeted cordially in a flat and nasal southern accent. "And whom may I have the pleasure of dining with this evening?"

"Thomas Simpson," I said. We shook hands. His grip was firm, aggressive. He looked me straight in the eye, a look of filial camaraderie, as if we were blood brothers who shared a very amusing secret. I could see how Gunderson had been a success.

"Now Thomas, what brings you into this august company of egomaniacal twits?"

"I'm the incoming director of campaign and university communications. Doing a presentation of the master plan for communications at tomorrow's meeting."

"Ah, yes! Pleasure to meet you, young man. Looking forward to your presentation." He reached out, cupped a hand behind my shoulder, pulled me closer and said conspiratorially, "Promise you won't put me to sleep!"

"Uh... not my intent. I've stashed a nude halfway through my power point. See if you catch it."

"Hah! I like it!"

A mischievous expression came to his face and suddenly he reached around me and grabbed a substantial piece of my right butt cheek in his hand and gave it a hard squeeze.

I jumped in surprise. "Jesus!" I exclaimed, looking around to see whether others had witnessed my assault. Apparently not. "God damn! Whatdayah think you're doing?"

"Ah, no big deal," Gunderson said, laughing hard. "Let's have some dinner."

I found myself glaring at him as he sat down but, after a moment of consideration, it seemed that there were really no options but to do the same. It was not my place to challenge his behavior, which was probably, I reflected, why it continued. At some point, somewhere, in a less prominent setting the redoubtable Allan Gunderson was going to get punched out.

"So you were in the bond trading business?" I asked Gunderson to make conversation as we waited for the table to fill.

"Well, yes, we was small potatahs..." he paused, "but we was good potatahs." He began to laugh at his own joke, his face turning crimson. I found I was laughing with him, hoping too that he was not about to stroke out or infarct. "But then we got gobbled up by Morgan Stanley and it made me a very rich man."

"Congratulations."

"Thank you, Thomas."

Bryan Fitz-Hugh stopped behind us as he walked by on the way to the head table. Put his hand on Gunderson's shoulder.

"Allan is totally out of the box," he said to me. "But we need that."

"Well, Bryan, at least I ain't outta the closet!"

"You've got to love this guy," Fitz-Hugh said, slapping

Gunderson on the back, "but I live in fear of what the hell is he going to say next." He shook his head in mock disapproval and left us.

Provost Kravitz approached our table, saw me and said, "Ah, neophyte, it is so good to see you. I'm so looking forward to your presentation," leaving the impression that it was decidedly not good to see me and that he meant to savage my presentation at the first convenience. Thankfully he sat on the other side. A few moments later our public relations director, John Fein, arrived in his normal state of barely contained panic and took his place next to Kravitz. Then Ursula arrived to sit on his other side. As she sat, she gave me a meaningful glance that conveyed the sacrifice she was making. But then she greeted Kravitz with great enthusiasm as if she was delighted to be his dinner partner.

Gunderson leaned over toward me. "I see the provost is a good friend of yours," he said in a half whisper.

"Yeah."

"He strikes me as the kinda guy whose skivvies are maybe a couple sizes too small. Got a permanent wedgie." He began to laugh uncontrollably at his own joke, his eyes watering.

I looked around the room.

Bernie Reve was sitting between the two CEO's, the three of them laughing uproariously at a joke he had just told. I found myself shaking my head.

Fitz-Hugh at the head table was sitting next to Mark Berger and having what appeared to be a flirtatious conversation with Maggie Garnet on his other side. Of course, I thought, his wife, Celeste, would not be here.

I felt a hand on my left leg and turned to see my other dinner partner, Ms. Fontaine, had arrived and was regarding me predatorily.

Her face was hawkish, her eyes small, active, flintlike. Her hair was close cut, light gray. Her promiscuous mouth was coated with red lipstick. She wore large jade encrusted earrings, a power necklace of agates and platinum and a slithery and sparkling jade colored dress.

"Hello young man," she pronounced in a husky baritone as she removed her hand and searched fruitlessly in a small glittering handbag looking for a light. She found a silver case and pulled from it an impossibly long and thin almost black cigarillo, tapped it on the table and looked back to me hopefully.

"I don't smoke."

She gazed at me flatly with a 'What good are you?' expression.

"Beatrice," Allan Gunderson said from my other side, "Be my guest." He tossed a book of bar matches across to her.

"Ah, my dear man, you are a life saver! Thank you!" she exclaimed. And then whispered to me, "And a terrible misogynist and homophobe.... And you are?"

"Thomas Simpson, director of communications."

She nodded, lit her cigarillo and blew a heavy wad of blue smoke away from the table, then turned back to me.

"Yes, my dear," she said, "a vile habit but I must admit one that I can't seem to get rid of. I hope you don't mind."

"Of course not."

"Well, you may say that, but it's clear that you do, and frankly, I must tell you that I don't give a shit. Get over it, love."

"Okay."

I felt Gunderson tugging at my arm and turned toward him.

"How'd you like to come home to that gargoyle every night?" he whispered. "Seriously, though, one smart lady. You'll see. Just lock your doors this evening. She's on the prowl."

"I can see you two get along famously."

Gunderson snorted in surprise, "Actually we do."

I felt Ms. Fontaine's hand on my leg again and turned to her.

She nodded slightly across the table to Kravitz.

"O, beware, my lord, of jealousy; It is the green-ey'd monster, which doth mock The meat it feeds on."

"Very good," I said.

"Othello, but you wouldn't know that, would you, darling?"

"No."

"Communications is an odd discipline. Devoid of culture, isn't it?"

"I'm afraid so."

As we were finishing the first course, Mark Berger's tapping of his fork against fine crystal brought our conversations to an abrupt halt.

He stood, white wine glass in hand. "Yah know, as I've told many of you, my accountants keep making me buy these places. Good tax dodge and all that. I always resist. But in this case, they flew me down to Miami, drove me out here and I took one look around this property and I called my main numbers guy, Ziggy. I said, 'Ziggy, where the hell do I sign? This is paradise!!!' So, welcome! You'll now understand why I'm often absent from some of our winter board meetings, hidin' out as I do in the meagre confines of the boat house. It's tough to leave this place!... Our staff stands ready and willing to assist you, so please do not hesitate to ask them for anything at all. I hope you enjoy your stay here." He raised his glass, "To our university and to our remarkable president, Bryan Fitz-Hugh, to my fellow board members, our academic team and the dedicated professionals who work tirelessly to help our university and to our successful meeting tomorrow."

We applauded.

Berger turned to Fitz-Hugh. "Bryan..." he queried and sat down as Fitz-Hugh stood.

"My commendations, Mark. You've been holding out on us. Henceforth I shall recommend that we designate your winter residence here as our southern campus and hold all winter board meetings here."

"Great idea Bryan," Berger smirked, "but we're booked! You're always welcome on the yacht however."

"What a unique property," Fitz-Hugh continued, "and how good and generous of you to host our board meeting. This is a place where we can relax, get to know one another a little better than we can in the faster-paced circumstances that normally surround these meetings. As well, we can take the time as a board to focus on the opportunities and challenges ahead. Let us raise our glasses to our beneficent host!"

With this final toast, dinner was served and the noise rose under the tent. Evening spread across the ocean turning it into a mauve pastel, stars beginning to come out and a cooler breeze moving through the tent.

It was not that I did not know the trick of dinner table conversation was to get those next to you to talk about themselves. Unfortunately, no matter how deftly I tried to turn the conversation around Gunderson kept grilling me in a very pleasant and inquisitive manner about Janet and our two kids and Ms. Fontaine managed to do the same about the communications master plan. I barely touched my dinner before it was whisked away and a replaced by a lemon parfait which looked wonderful but by this point of my inquisition was completely unappetizing.

As for Kravitz and Ursula, he actually seemed to warm to her blandishments. I felt a small, distracted pang of jealously but was too busy dealing with the conversations to either side of me during the rest of dinner to give their exchange much further thought.

Finally, we all rose to leave. I watched Ursula and Kravitz walk toward the president's table.

"I must go," Ms. Fontaine said importantly and then placed a hand on my arm and looked directly into my eyes, "but I do hope we can spend some time together tomorrow."

"Sure."

She turned and strolled back into the hotel.

"Thomas," Gunderson said from behind me.

"Yeah," I turned.

"Pleasure meeting you, young man." We shook hands. "Don't worry about tomorrow. I'll have your back. I know Berger will too. We've been talking."

"Thanks, Allan. That sure beats you having my ass."

Gunderson laughed. "Oh, I don't know about that, son. Good ass is hard to find! I'm headed to the bar. Care to join me? I believe Frank Lusby and Bernie Reve will be there."

"No, I've got to get some sleep."

"Suit yourself. See you in the mornin'."

"You got it."

Later, I lay in bed in the dark looking out of the balcony's open doors at the moonlight on the ocean.

The handle on the room door made a faint sound as its knob was turned carefully. Ursula entered the room silently, undressed, slithered under the sheet and we embraced.

"I thought I would never get free," she whispered in an exasperated tone.

"Yeah, I wondered."

"Our president is with Mrs. Garnet. That is the only reason why I could get away."

"Oh, Jesus. A supreme sacrifice for our alma mater."

She laughed ruefully, "Oh yes."

"Why did you put me between those two? Lord, Gunderson got me in the ass and Ms. Fontaine about devoured me for dinner. I think she wore a hole in my pants from stroking my leg."

"I thought you would find them interesting."

"Bullshit. You thought it was funny. And then you sit across from me flirting with Kravitz. I thought I was going to puke."

"Yes." Ursula began to laugh. "And it was very funny to watch you have to deal with them while I was entertaining the provost, man eater on one side, ass grabber on the other."

"Hilarious."

I got out of bed, closed the balcony doors carefully and pulled the curtains closed.

"We'll need to be really quiet," I said getting back into bed.

"Yes."

V

A Little White Lie

T he Bishop was a woman of grace and humility, strength and conviction, who inspired programs to help those in need, a woman who loved her family dearly, who told life lessons, often humorous, from her experiences serving in different countries and from her present raising of three sons and a daughter, a woman who was savvy politically and whose awareness seemed at times to extend beyond our worldly realm.

Stories about this latter trait circulated about the diocese. How she could greet people she had met in crowded circumstances years before and recall their name and their prior conversation. How, when entering her office or in her presence during services, one could sense an unexplained aura. How she seemed to intuit family crises and call at the perfect time. Some wondered whether their experiences with her involved clerical parlor tricks... or... were they something else?

During my time at the diocese I did not work directly for the Bishop but reported to her second-in-command, the Suffragan Bishop, Hanley Harris, a very different personality, in some ways complementary, in others not. While the Bishop was the spiritual, religious leader of the diocese, Harris in addition to his clerical duties as second-in-command, was its chief operating officer. Therefore, given that I was the director of development, a title given to the head fund raising professional, I reported to Bishop Harris rather than the presiding Bishop.

Harris, a former executive, had seen the light of his faith illuminate at a late age, had joined the ministry in his thirties and worked his way up the ladder assiduously through his commanding competency and an ability to also turn on at the right moments a personality. He was a man who wore many hats and who had many switches. As his underling, I had to be very careful to know which of his hats or switches were on or off before broaching any particular subject because on a daily basis Harris served the diocese and its operations with all the zeal of a laser-vision cyborg terminator. Woe be the vendor, staffer or congregant who ran afoul of the Suffragan Bishop when the COO switch was on and the Harris laser beam of disapproval fell upon them and they were effectively vaporized, at least in a spiritual sense. So, part of my job was to keep Harris on an even keel and as much as possible keep his clerical and humanistic switches on and his cyborg executive switch off.

A further underlying difficulty was the simple fact that Bishop Harris lusted after the presiding Bishop's position. This was apparent to all of us, but our awareness was not apparent to Hanley himself. Executives, it seemed to me, those in charge, often through the isolation of authority, developed tone deafness and blind spots.

When it came to fund raising, we had unique challenges. The Bishop was charming but viewed her relationships with her congregants as pastoral and therefore could not be easily convinced to make a request for support. Harris, on the other hand, was all too motivated to make requests for support but was utterly unaware of any need for personal relationships and their accompanying nuances. My job was the choreography of our approaches to top prospects and donors, so I was continually trying to persuade the Bishop about how she might engage them without compromising her pastoral relationship while also trying to persuade Harris on the correct strategy and role he needed to play to develop meaningful friendships.

"Hanley," I would tell him, "You can't walk up to someone or have lunch with them and just announce how much the diocese would like them to contribute. You have to draw them out over time, get them talking about their interests and passions, the programs or other interests that light up their lives. And then share with them what the plans are for those things they're particularly attracted to, make them part of the planning process, bring them in, get them involved until the role they might play in the future of this place becomes apparent to both of you. Then you'll be having a conversation about how they could, as part of the diocesan family, be part of our legacy to coming generations."

There were also circumstantial challenges that confronted us.

The first being a complication: whom do bishops talk to about their concerns or worries, challenges and opportunities without diminishing their relationship, respect or authority? Think about it. Other bishops? Not likely. Family? They couldn't possibly understand the complexity of politics in a diocese. The Lord? Not a lot of feedback from that quarter.

As it turns out, our bishop, for whatever reasons, found a ready ear and an assurance of confidentiality in the diocese's chief fund raiser, *moi*. Once a month or so, the internal line in my office would ring and the Bishop would invite me to an off campus lunch, usually at a small, delightfully upscale nearby French restaurant of such expense and such privacy that for all practical purposes we were assured that we would not be discovered.

There over a glass of wine and a memorable meal the Bishop would ask about my family, how we and the children were faring and would happily discuss her own family's progress or challenges, minor worries and concerns. I would listen too as the Bishop told me about her life, interests, goings on in the diocese and in particular her concerns about Hanley Harris and his overweening ambition. There was a moment toward the end of one of our delightful lunches where she placed a hand softly on the table, looked at me directly, and said, "You understand, of course, that Hanley will never be Bishop." She paused to let this sink in, and then intoned, an emphasis on each word, "He has no grace."

It felt to me at that moment that it was the Lord who was speaking through the Bishop, not the Bishop herself.

Caught between a rock, my loyalty to the Bishop, and a hard place, my duty to my direct superior, I knew without a doubt that should Hanley ever learn of my confidential lunches with the Bishop I one way or another would be terminated.

We had at that time an ongoing capital campaign for endowment. As part of that effort, we also had an erstwhile, periodic, high-priced fund-raising consultant from the so-called Mercedes-Benz of consulting firms whose track record with diocesan fund raising was august and without compare, at least according to them. Our consultant, Seymour Ruble – yes, that was his real name - visited us monthly, huddled with the Bishop, huddled with Hanley Harris, met in private with the board of trustees of the diocese and then visited my office where, thankfully, he collegially disgorged all that he had learned. Together we would then figure out what next steps and strategies should be taken going forward.

I told my family upon first meeting him how ironic it seemed to me that our consulting firm would assign a Jewish consultant to a Protestant account. Maybe that's what they thought we needed, I surmised, the United Jewish Appeal approach in the land of the frozen chosen.

In any case, Sammie, as he called himself, was a short man with rumpled black hair and rumpled black suits, scuffed up black shoes, white shirts with dry cleaner folds in them, food stained ties and a face drawn with the hyper charm and irritability that often accompanies alcoholism. Lord knows, he was funny. I never knew what the hell was going to come out of his mouth. In times of stress, which was most of time, he had a severe tic, a snapping closing and opening of his eyes, more of a spasm than a blink, that interrupted him mid-speech and was a grave distraction to any conversation.

It was Sammie who had revealed to me a deep, dark secret: the diocese was for all intents and purposes insolvent. Not through any fault of the current administration but because under the previous bishop the board of trustees had authorized the borrowing of tens of millions from the endowment to finance the expansion of facilities and ministry among its various parishes - a flexing of diocesan muscle and the purchasing of obeisance. All done before any of my, the Bishop's or Hanley's time, through the assurances of the previous bishop to the board that he knew of several very substantial bequests that would shortly be coming the diocese's way. They had accepted his assertions on good faith.

One of the first things I had done, at Hanley's request, was search for any documentation we had regarding these bequests. There was none.

The previous bishop had been consulted. With the clueless geniality that occasionally accompanies early dementia, he happily named names. Most of those named were dead. No bequests had been forthcoming. Hanley very carefully and confidentially contacted the others the former bishop cited. No, we were not in their estate plans.

What we also discovered belatedly, since the diocese's financial records were in disarray, and what Hanley found only after numerous late nights with his accounting hat on, is that with the evisceration of a significant portion of the endowment and its annual payout and with the added annual expense of new ministry programs, the diocese was now short over one-third of its yearly budget. As a final blow, Hanley then discovered that the former administration had been funding the annual operating deficit through further dipping into the endowment without knowledge or permission of the board, an act which they had referred to in their slipshod record keeping as 'internal borrowing'.

This was reported in deep confidence and chagrin to the board of trustees.

Hanley had been directed to cut staff, which did not help his growing laser beam reputation.

A confidential line of credit had been garnered from a prominent local bank on whose board several of the diocese's board of trustee members served.

And, of course, our fundraising consulting firm was hired and the capital campaign for endowment was cobbled together rapidly and launched to great publicity and fanfare, no mention being made that the endowment funds raised would be replacing those that had been spent or that gifts to the campaign not specifically designated to endowment would fund our annual operating deficit and bank loan interest.

So, our campaign was built on a foundation of lies. Not what I had signed up for but I found myself feeling a profound need to support our bishop in these trying times and so stayed on despite daily misgivings.

But Sammie, as our high-priced consultant, assured us that he had a plan to save the day.

The Bishop had developed a meaningful relationship with a couple who were vastly wealthy through their marriage of inheritance and self-made fortunes, individuals who lived on an estate in the country of thousands of acres and who had four other homes around the world but who had taken a particular liking to the Bishop, held her in the highest regard and would on occasion attend her services. Recently, they had come to her with a problem. Their local country parish was searching for a new rector and the candidates who had surfaced were not at all the right fit. Could she help?

The Bishop had taken their request under consideration and behind the scenes had reached out to a colleague of many years, secured his interest and presented his credentials to the couple. Long story short, their parish hired her recommendation, who by all reports had been very well received, and the couple had showered the Bishop with their appreciation, praise and some modest gifts in her honor.

Sammie saw in them a redemption for the diocese and success for the capital campaign. They would be presented with the opportunity to support their bishop in her effort to raise endowment funds through a lead endowment gift of tens of millions to the capital campaign. There was some logical and considered justification for this given their prior eight and nine figure generosity to their alma maters and to arts and cultural organizations. Plus, all our research and wealth screenings indicated a remarkable capacity for future philanthropy.

Preparations began. The Bishop was persuaded, against her better instincts but recognizing that our backs were against a wall, to set a meeting with them at the downtown townhouse they used as offices for their foundation and personal philanthropy.

Sammie and I worked up a script of talking points for the Bishop, whose role would be to discuss the uplifting impact a significant lead endowment gift would have on the diocese, its parishes, people and programs, how it would inspire and encourage other lead donors and prospects, while Hanley would discuss how such a gift would be handled internally and to answer any other questions regarding the endowment, accounting, investment, diocesan operations, campaign publicity or anonymity.

With great fanfare, Sammie showed up at my office with a beautiful leather portfolio in which we inserted on thick vellum a summary of the Bishop's and Suffragan

Bishop's talking points for review with the couple. This to forestall any attempt to wander from their script and be sure the couple had a hard copy for later review of what was to be discussed.

The day of the meeting arrived. Sammie was out of town on another assignment, so it was left to me to brief the Bishop and Hanley. The three of us sat around a coffee table in an alcove in the Bishop's office, early morning sunlight pouring in on us through the surrounding leaves, the ancient, stone building quiet, the bishop wearing her clerical collar, a purple smock, a large ornate cross pendant gracing it, black skirt and dress coat, Hanley in a gray suit, black clerical shirt and collar, as I reviewed with them their talking points which were typed up on a single piece of stationery each of them would carry in their personal portfolios.

I felt a certain degree of helplessness as I ushered them out the door for their drive downtown. Then I trudged back up the stairs to my office and busied myself with returning emails and phone calls and with paperwork. In what seemed like only minutes, but in checking my watch I discovered had been an hour and a half, I heard some commotion and conversation on the stairs and realized that it was the Bishop and Hanley returning from their visit.

They traipsed into my office and before they even took seats in front of my desk I was alarmed. Collectively, everything about them, from their gait to their clothes to their facial expressions looked as if they had experienced a nearby lightning strike, eyebrows seemingly askew, clerical collars slightly off center, Hanley's suit and the bishop's purple smock and black dress coat as if they had slept in them, heads tilted at strange angles, hair out of place. Worse, I could see that the Bishop was carrying the leather portfolio that Sammie and I had worked so hard to prepare tucked under her arm.

"Um, how'd it go?" I asked as they sat and looked as me as if they were about to endure a graduate oral exam.

"Delightful meeting," the Bishop opined, "They are such a gracious couple."

I looked over at Hanley. He looked baleful and guilty. I thought, *Shit!*

"And the campaign, their gift?"

The Bishop looked at me blankly, as if my question had not registered, looked over at Hanley, who was looking at the floor. Then realized she needed to say something.

"It's the strangest thing," she remarked.

"It is?"

"They didn't realize that we were having an endowment campaign. It was all news to them. Hanley and I discussed this on our return drive. Despite all the publicity, articles in the diocesan newsletters and magazine, press releases, letters sent to them, they travel so much, are out of the country a good deal, they must have missed it all."

"Oh, my God."

"Yes," the Bishop agreed. "Quite awkward."

"So, what in the hell did you talk about?"

There was a pause. The Bishop and Hanley looked at one another. "Well," the Bishop told me, "We caught up with one another, with our families and with their recent travels and plans for the coming months. And then we did talk about the diocese and our plans for the future and the endowment campaign, but... it seemed very inappropriate to talk about their making a lead gift to an effort they were just learning about..." She paused without finishing her thought.

I sighed, "Well, I agree with you there. So, how did you leave things?"

"Oh," the Bishop told me, "I'll follow up with a phone call to thank them for their time and see whether we might meet again when we can brief them in more detail about our needs and the campaign." But there was little conviction in her assertion. How long would it take for that to happen? Would she even make the call?

"Ohhh..." I heard myself sigh disappointedly. "Okay." The whole effort with our prospective lead donors seemed dead in the water.

We all went our separate ways and I spent most of the next week examining daily the paltry spreadsheet of our campaign's attainment to date and shaking my head.

I did call Sammie and gave him a brief version of what had happened.

"They fucking fucked up!" he half-yelled.

"It's a little more complicated than that. In any case, should we ever get another opportunity like this, I'll send materials on the campaign in advance with a handwritten note from the Bishop and call in advance to make sure they've received them, ask whether they have any questions."

There was a long pause on the line, and then Sammie's voice came back to me, contrite and quilt ridden, "Yeah, well maybe I fucked up too, you know."

"Yeah."

"You don't necessarily have to agree with me!"

"Hey, we all take the blame on this one. Team effort."

"Yeah. Okay. Gotta go."

Then toward the week's end I received a call from the Bishop.

"We're in luck," she told me. "They're still in town. I've set a meeting for Monday at their townhouse."

She paused for a long moment. "The last meeting. Hanley was quite somber, funeral."

"Oh, damn. He was wearing the wrong hat."

"Pardon?"

"Never mind."

"He was very off-putting. So much so that they kept looking over at him while we talked, as if they were concerned he was becoming ill. Very distracting. So, I've decided that it is best if he does not accompany me for this next meeting."

"He'll be furious."

"Rather than keep my meeting from him – he would find out about it sooner or later and, yes, would be quite upset – I called him and... well... told him a little white lie, that our friends actually called me about a pastoral matter and that while meeting with them I would try my best to again address the campaign."

"Okayyyy... How'd he take that?"

"He was, of course, not happy but he did seem to understand and accept their need."

It was no longer than ten minutes before my phone rang again with Hanley asking that I meet with him ASAP.

I put on my game face of naivete and ignorance, mixed in what I hoped was a dollop of stupidity and descended to Suffragan Bishop's office.

Hanley was at his desk, his expression full of consternation.

"I talked with the Bishop earlier and she's meeting again with our best prospects on Monday."

"That's great news."

"Well, I'm not so sure. They've called and asked for the meeting. It's of a pastoral nature."

"Oh..."

"The Bishop assures me that she will do her best to turn the conversation around to the campaign if there is any opportunity to do so."

"Well, I'll cross my fingers."

Hanley paused, his forehead wrinkled up. "I'm deeply concerned for them. I will pray for them."

"That serious?"

"Yes. It staggers my imagination that a couple so blessed with wealth and attainment would have marital issues."

"Really?"

"Yes. Now you must keep this in complete confidence."

"Of course."

"He apparently wants to take up sky diving and she apparently wants to have another child. They're fighting like cats and dogs."

"They're in their sixties!" I exclaimed, playing my part as best I could, my shock at the brazen audaciousness of the Bishop's 'little white lie' and at Hanley's gullibly infusing my reaction.

"Yes. Isn't that amazing? To me, it illustrates that no matter how much wealth and success people have, so often they can never be satisfied. We of faith know the error of their ways. I fervently hope the Bishop can turn their attention to their faith and to their salvation. Surely, if anyone could show them in an inspiring manner the error of their ways, it would be her."

"Yes, I certainly agree. I'm sure the Bishop would be pleased to hear you say that."

"We all know she is very gifted."

"Nevertheless, I think it would be most difficult to turn the conversation from their salvation to making a significant, lead endowment gift to the diocese."

"Yes. It would take a miracle."

The remainder of the week and weekend passed slowly.

The following Monday, late in the afternoon, when I was about to give up all hope of hearing from the Bishop, she called and asked me to meet with her and Hanley in her office.

Again, as I tried to minimize the noise of my galloping footsteps down the stairs, I put on my game face to assure I would in no way reveal Hanley's shared confidence of the Bishop's fabrication.

She was sitting with Hanley at the coffee table in the alcove, late afternoon sun illuminating the space. I took a seat, glanced at both of them. She was quite composed; Hanley was a bundle of nerves.

"We had a good and productive meeting," she told us. "Once we worked through their issues and concerns, we actually had a very pleasant conversation about the campaign. I was able to communicate its purpose and needs and what it would mean to me and the diocese if they might consider a lead role."

"Did you ask for a specific amount?" I blurted.

"Well, no. I asked that they pray on it and that they do their best."

"Oh..."

"What is our follow-up?" Hanley asked, not doing any better job at concealing his disappointment than I.

"They promised they would consider my request and get back to me in the near future."

Hanley and I were speechless.

"Okay..." I said finally. "Do you want me to write a follow-up note for them?"

"No, I think I should do that, reflecting on our conversation and their consideration of my request."

"Okay..."

No word came from our couple. The campaign continued, slowly at first and then gradually it picked up momentum.

In the end, after a long, convoluted two more years, the faithful rose to the challenge of our need and we were successful, ironically in part because of several actual bequests.

As we prepared for the victory celebration, we receive a gift of stock from the couple we had so inexpertly solicited at the beginning of our effort. The gift was approximately one-twentieth the amount we had outlined in our leather portfolio proposal to them. Still a meaningful amount and done in appreciation for the Bishop and for the success of our capital campaign.

When I called Sammie to tell him of the gift, he exclaimed, "Ah, see, we didn't fuck up. Wouldn't ah mattered what we did or didn't do, the diocese just isn't a priority. Never will be. So, it wasn't our fault, after all. I hear they just made a pledge of another $100 mil to his university. Well, that's the way it goes, win some, lose some. But it all turned out okay, right?"

I thought about Hanley, now with his chin up and his chest puffed out with pride at the campaign's success, marching around the premises in an *Onward Christian Soldiers* manner, about the rumors that he was a candidate for bishop in three other dioceses.

I thought about the Bishop who was, as ever, graceful and politic in all she did, happy that her children were succeeding at school, that the diocese was fiscally healthy again, that she now had time to shepherd new programs to combat hunger and to have inner city parishes open their doors to provide a safe haven for after school, latch key kids, serving her Lord faithfully.

I thought about the fact that I was still at my job, the miracle of it all perhaps being that Hanley had not yet discovered the Bishop and my friendship and terminated me.

"Yeah," I replied, "I guess in a way, it did."

VI

No One Talks

With great care Charlie Day placed his fingertips on the opposite sides of the sweating vodka and tonic on the linen tablecloth in front of him. He examined the drink through his thick glasses, as if the drowned lime at its bottom could reveal the meaning of life, before he looked up at me with a knowing expression and said, "Craig, I've heard confession again."

"Oh, hell," I told him, "please don't start with another of these."

His eyebrows arched slightly in mock innocence. "But why?"

"Because, Charlie, it's not fair telling me things I can't write a column about. It just makes me frustrated..."

Charlie looked down at his drink and stuck out his lower lip, considering this.

"So talk..." I said.

He picked a rye roll out of the breadbasket, examined it with equal care, broke it open, picked up his butter knife, speared a hard square from the ice within the silver butter dish and began mashing it into the ragged middle.

Charlie was my college roommate, and we had been

for many years the best of friends. Over the last decade, however, our friendship had faded and had turned us into mildly affectionate footnotes in one another's lives. I am not sure why -- perhaps friendships, like wind-up toys, wear out after a time, or maybe it was that our wives saw the two of us together as too exclusive of them. Whatever it was, the extent of our relationship now was that we lunched on very occasional Fridays and traded insults, information, and confidences, for after all these years one final therapeutic certainty remained -- no one talked.

"As you know," Charlie began, "my great boss, friend and mentor, the senator, is very big on self-help. So, over the last several years, he's managed to establish a non-profit foundation to provide start-up challenge grants to grass roots organizations whose aim is to develop self-help entrepreneurial programs in disadvantaged neighborhoods. The whole idea has absolutely brilliant PR dimensions to it."

"How do you mean?"

"Oh, come on. Think for a second. From the senator's viewpoint he can buy votes by making small grants to community organizations in areas where he wants support. He gets lots of local recognition, good press, a national reputation as a philanthropist, idea man, a real leader. Plus, anyone who thinks they or their organization might get some money is going to vote for him."

"Uh, so where's the money coming from, Charlie?"

"Oh," said he innocently, "from the senator's many friends."

"Like the usual developers, PAC's, corporations, billionaires and unions?"

"Like I said, many friends.

"As it turns out, the first $5,000 grant went to a home town apartment complex tenants' association which had become so disenchanted with the management of its complex that they wanted to take it over.

"No repairs were being performed. There were drug dealers all over the place. As a result few people were paying rent. So the tenants' association, feeling the city wasn't giving them any help in their fight against the scumbag owners, pooled their nickels and dimes and sent their president to Washington. The senator saw the woman, who is one dedicated, sharp lady, and decided to give the association a grant from his foundation to help it with mobilization expenses. I thought it was a gutsy move and went along with it, although I warned the senator of the potential for backfire."

"Did it?" I asked.

"No way. This tenant association came through like you would not believe. First, they visited every unit and enlisted tenant support, began collecting back rent and placed it in escrow as leverage. They used that as a bargaining tool to force the owner to begin repairs on the units. They also began negotiations on actually purchasing the complex and having it tenant-managed. They formed volunteer teams of skilled and semi-skilled people to begin making additional repairs and to clean up. They have asked the owner to consider a contract in which the association's repairmen would perform most apartment maintenance. This would allow lower costs and assure that the work was done by people who cared. As well, the association would profit and could do more.

"They formed their own security force and went to the police and said if the police didn't clean up the drug dealers, they would. As a result, their complex is off limits to dealers. They're talking about day care and tutorial projects for their kids if their repair and maintenance contract is accepted. Now other people are fighting to rent there. The tenants' association had an auction/flea market that was so successful they netted not only the matching funds but also enough that they even <u>paid</u> <u>back</u> the initial $5,000 grant. The publicity has been unbelievable. Everyone wins on this one, and particularly the senator.

"Needless to say, our fine senator was more than a little pumped up by this experience. In his mind, it was time to go national and build even greater acclaim. So he went to a major foundation, which shall remain nameless except that it has several hundred million in assets, and to two state corporations and secured grants totaling $650,000. He set his wife, Marla, up as president of the foundation and generated even more publicity as well as about 10,000 grant applications."

I shrugged. "Sounds great."

"That's what I, as a good, loyal aide de camp, thought. Great publicity. National reputation. Everyone loves him back home. Political leverage being gained through the grant-making process. Can cut some good deals with that. Don't spend any of our own money. Perfectly legal. Senator's one step removed because his wife heads the deal. That looks good for her as a concerned citizen. Further, it gets Marla out of my hair."

"So, what's the problem?"

Charlie looked down at his drink again as a rueful,

small smile edged itself onto his features. Finally, he said, "They spent it."

Our waiter came and we ordered lunch, and when he left, for a few moments we watched one another's little boy grins.

"The $650,000?" I asked.

"Yeah."

"Holy shit! On what?"

"Themselves."

"Oh, terrific."

"That's about what I thought, except there were maybe four expletives between the 'Oh' and the 'terrific.'"

"So how did you find out?"

"Two weeks ago, I'm in my office cranking out a press release at seven in the evening, wondering why I keep doing this, and like he always does, the senator came schlepping in with this big guilty look on his face like he just cheated on a math test, which I'm sure he did with regularity as a child. And he says, 'Can we talk?'

"I took one long look at him and called Mary and said, 'I'll be a while,' and I could tell she knew exactly what I meant -- maybe a couple of weeks."

"What the hell did they spend it on?"

Charlie shrugged. "Time share in Vail, some bad stock, Mercedes SUV. Hell, $650,000 doesn't go very far these days.... Anyway, so the senator says, 'Charlie, what do I do?'

"I hadn't exactly formed a strategy, but I sensed immediately that the solution, at least on a cash-needed basis, had to be back in the district, away from the smaller town and the bigger gossip and the thousands lobbyists and you journalists in Washington. Further, as I'm sure you are aware, there are few real friends in this town or anyone decent and naive enough to provide good faith assistance. So I called the airport, booked a flight, called in an intern and had him start canceling everything for the next few days because of a 'family emergency,' called a limo and we were off. I mean, I figured we'd better move our asses fast."

"Who knew about this?"

"Just Marla. . . . The problem is, they got to thinking it was their money. There were a whole bunch of start-up and administrative costs for the foundation, and somehow that got construed by them as providing discretionary power over the funds. They were thinking that they would spend the money now and just raise a whole lot more later, award the grants and no one would be the wiser. Now there was the senator, a damned fine attorney, or used to be before he got Potomac Fever, and he was not even thinking clearly enough to realize that they have got to file a full list of expenditures and that the IRS is currently scrutinizing the activities of small foundations. I mean, I think the guy has blown some diodes somewhere. The information goes in these days, but it's not being synthesized like it used to be. We are probably damned lucky Marla didn't find a line of credit somewhere.

"Oh, yeah, you know what else they did? They bought a sailboat. The idea was it was a good capital investment with good depreciation. Nice touch. I told him they should christen the damn thing *Going Down!*

"Anyway, on the flight out to his district, I said to the senator, 'Look . . . can you tell me as accurately as you can about your current assets and liabilities.'

"He said, 'Oh.... I don't know.... We're not in bad shape.'

"I mean, he didn't even connect with why I was asking.

"So I ordered a couple of drinks and filled in with some light talk about football and the clean air act and after the second round I said, 'Senator, I have got to know about your liabilities and assets to find out where there is enough cash or credit or collateral available to pay back the money you have illegally expropriated from your foundation.'

"He said, 'Oh...'

"So, the senator begins to lay out salary and assets and debts and I'm adding them up in two columns, and let me tell you, Column B, Liabilities, is lavish. I mean, they are so deep in hock that any normal human would infarct. I mean, they are making $650,000 a year and their *mortgage* is over three mil. Both kids are in private school. They got a BMW SUV, the new Mercedes and country club membership and a yearly vacation and a housekeeper. I mean, I'm thinking, 'How is this guy <u>not</u> on the take?' It's no damn wonder they spent the assets of the foundation. Spending is *all* the hell they know how to do.

"So then the senator started talking sort of poor mouth about his responsibilities -- his kids and Marla and his mother, who's senile and lives in this big house and requires round the clock nursing, who they thought was going to die a few years ago and leave them some money, except she never did.

"I asked, 'Is your mother's house paid for?'

"The senator looked sort of startled, and he says, 'Well... yeah... sure.'

"'Are you executor of the estate, with power of attorney?' I asked.

"He looked horrified for a moment or two and then

gradually kind of beaten, and he answered weakly, 'Yeah, I guess so.'

"'You figure your mother's house is worth at least million?' I asked him.

"'Yeah...' he answered.

"'You remember Mr. Atwater, that nice gentleman who was a big donor to your campaign who happens to be the president of First Interstate Bank?'

"'Yeah,' he said.

"'Well,' I said, 'We're going to go visit him tomorrow morning. Let's hope to God he's in. We'll get a loan on your mother's house for the balance of your debt to the foundation and refund the foundation with a wire transfer. Then we'll fly back to Washington and talk with a financial planner friend of mine who will be more than happy to take you on as a client. He'll make you sell your sailboat and some of your other things, and he'll put you on an allowance for a few years until you've funded this debt. You'll probably have to do away with your housekeeper, the private schools and country club. I want you to have Marla bring all the foundation documentation and particularly the checkbook to me. I'm going to explain to her that from this point forward I'll serve as foundation administrator. We can maintain her as president and she can control grant decisions based on my control of assets. Further, you'd better explain to her that you can't fire me because I know too much and because, with the help of a former IRS attorney friend of mine, I'm going to figure out some ingenious transfer scheme to get all these transactions looking clean, fresh and separate. You might tell her, too, that I'm trying to help you guys even though you both won't like me very much.'"

"So what happened?"

"Oh, it all went beautifully. Marla was better than I thought, mainly because she's scared. In a couple of years, as soon as they feel they're out of trouble, I'll gradually lose my position on the staff, and if I stick around I'll be squeezed out."

"That's cynical."

"That's correct."

"Probably."

"Yeah."

I smiled at him. "And no one talks."

Charlie smiled back. "No one."

VII

Sandhill Crane Estates

Mid-morning on a crisp, clear Florida west coast February day and Stanley Gruber, corpulent and bent from the waist by arthritis, walked toward the Sandhill Crane Estates gatehouse for his daily supervisory visit, his game face expression one of mean authority subtly laced with joy.

He wore his customary ancient, thin and yellowing V neck t-shirt untucked over old acrylic shorts of a brown-yellow hue not found in nature except perhaps on splattered windshields.

"Hey, Mr. G.!" Herman, the uniformed lead gatehouse guard, greeted him enthusiastically. Herman had been waiting for over an hour to make his morning report, but he would make no mention of this.

Gruber was a member of the community association board, currently holding no title, but make no mistake about it, he was in charge.

He and Herman entered the small, air-conditioned guard house. Gruber sat on a folding chair from his palatial home that he had permanently installed there.

"What's going on today, Herman?" Gruber demanded.

Herman picked his clipboard off the counter while

keeping an eye on the gate so that he could continue to monitor residents whose key fobs automatically gained them entrance while stopping for identification any guests, delivery trucks or workmen.

Sandhill Crane Estates was a golf community of three hundred and twenty-one houses twelve miles inland. Its website described it as "distinguished." In other words, a neighborhood populated by numerous physicians, retirees, car dealers, local family business owners, lawyers, bankers, realtors and families with husbands who commuted weekly to high powered jobs up north.

"Well, Mr. G., on my morning inspection, here's what I come up with:

"The Jensens are leaving their garbage cans outside in their drive again. Them cans are all messed up and broke too. Look like hell."

"Letter," Gruber commanded. "Covenant 11 clearly states that garbage cans have to be behind a fence or in the garage except for Monday trash pick-up. Have the management company send the one that starts with "Neighbors have complained..."

"Okay. The O'Malley's puppy was out in their front yard without a leash. I think Mrs. was getting the paper outta the drive while he was out there."

"That's the third time they have blatantly ignored the leash covenant. Call Animal Control."

"Sure thing."

"The Dennis's have guests in a camper van that's parked on the street and hasn't moved in a couple days."

"Notice in the mailbox that they are in violation of Covenant 14."

"Yes sir."

"The Moppetts just installed a new front door and painted that sucker red."

"Letter."

"The Smiths have put a sign in their yard endorsing Lombardi for mayor."

"Notice in their mailbox for immediate removal. Not to mention that he's a terrible choice."

"The Brundages, very sneaky, have left a for sale sign from last Sunday up against the house."

"Mailbox. No such signs are allowed on other days."

And so it went through another seven violations until Herman with some hesitancy brought up a situation he felt duty bound to report but where common sense told him he was treading on dangerous ground.

"So, uh... the Merskey residence. They're starting to lay out a foundation in the back of the yard."

Herman and Gruber looked at one another for confirmation of their mutual caution and uncertainty at the mention of this particular resident's name.

Salvatore Merskey lived in a massive Italianate stone house built on a natural sand ridge and surrounded by its own stone wall on its own lake at the outer edges of the community. It had been the first house built. Apparently, Mersky had at the time of his house's construction also bought up the hundreds of acres to the east. Some years later he had chosen a developer for this land and included his property as part of Sandhill Crane Estates incorporation. No one was really sure why he had done this. Taxes? A feudal wish to play king? In any case, his mansion's drive, which had its own electronic gate, flowed from the ridge on which the Mersky mansion was built into the main road of lowly Sandhill Crane Estates.

Many questioned how the neighborhood's developer had been chosen, whether in fact Merskey had some business relationship with him and what that might be. Where had the financing for the development come from for instance? One of the resident lawyers had done title searches at the courthouse and found no references to financing. It was all something of a mystery.

Further, no one knew what Merskey did or had done for a living which of course created any number of rumors about him. Limousines from various parts of the country routinely making visits to his house only added to the intrigue. Merskey was rarely seen, except for one incident that had taken place a number of years before at the Sandhill Crane Estates annual Halloween party, where Merskey had actually made an appearance. Driven there in his limousine, he had emerged, immaculately dressed in a white linen suit, a diminutive man in his late 70's. A realtor fueled by one too many plastic glasses of chardonnay upon being introduced had congratulated him, "Great gangster costume, man!"

Merskey had turned on his heel and left. The realtor had been chastised by his neighbors and friends and in the ensuing weeks everyone breathed a sigh of relief that nothing untoward had happened.

"Notice in the mailbox that they are in violation of Covenant 8 against any outbuildings."

"You really want to do that, Mr. G.?"

"Do it. Do it this morning. I want to nip this in the bud."

"Yes sir. If you don't mind my sayin' so, Mr. G. I don't

know what this neighborhood would do without you. I look at the things you and me gotta get straightened out each day and I think, 'Suppose you weren't here and this stuff went on unchecked?' Lord."

"Thank you, Herman. The association certainly appreciates the good job you are doing."

"Thank you, sir."

Walking back to his house Gruber felt his usual sense of accomplishment about the morning's corrective actions. However, on this occasion it was tainted by a nagging doubt about the Merskey situation. He reflected that nevertheless, it was a significant covenant that was being violated. You couldn't have outbuildings springing up all over the community.

Someone had to keep order or the place would be overrun by off leash dogs biting people not to mention owners letting them crap several times daily without cleaning up after them, garbage cans strewn about, houses painted god awful colors, rows of random mailboxes, boat trailers and camper vans strewn about, outbuildings the size of small houses, pick-up trucks in every drive and kids destructively skate boarding across important infrastructure and trespassing on his and everyone else's property. The next thing you knew the wrong element would move in and property values would go to hell.

When he reached his residence, Gruber stood outside for a moment admiring it from the street, arms folded across his chest.

It was a meticulously landscaped house, faced with a synthetic wood, painted an unsanctioned-by-community-covenants celadon green and located on what the community's developer had named "Placid Lake," actually a large pond carved out of the flat landscape to create elevation for the golf course.

This time of year the house looked particularly impressive. The hibiscus and oleanders were in bloom, the lavender of plumbago lined his walkways and his mighty Sylvester palms framed the house perfectly, his lawn closely cut and perfectly trimmed by his yard service.

Inside he changed then drove his Escalade to the Sandhill Crane Estates Golf and Country Club for his usual lunch at his usual table.

He loved the order and symmetry of his days, particularly lunch in this same spot in immaculate surroundings. He always sat at a table in the main dining room, away from the golfers who hung out in the grill. At this time of day there were just a few remnant bridge groups for lunch and no one around to bother him.

Cool waves from the air conditioning drifted down on him from the slow movement of the fans overhead. Outside, through the picture window, the emerald golf course and its sand traps and water hazards trailed away into the distance. As he carefully sipped his first martini, he swelled with pride and contentment as he surveyed his domain, knowing the important role he played in making it a civilized place in which to live.

It was a good life he had made for himself after all the stress of his earlier days running several dry-cleaning businesses in New Jersey, enduring the trials of a marriage to a woman who had grown to not appreciate him as a bread winner and companion. Finally, through divorce and his retirement he had gained his freedom and had had the good fortune to find this community.

He sighed a long sigh of contentment as his lunch arrived, ordered another martini and gazing again out the window almost smiled.

After lunch, he drove back down the street to his house, feeling a bit inebriated and drowsy, thinking that perhaps it was time for a nap. However, when his house came into view, he noticed with alarm that his sprinkler system was on, showering his lawn and shrubbery with an unscheduled deluge to the extent that the street gutters now ran with water from his property.

As small shots of panic went through him, he pulled the Escalade into the drive and walked briskly around the side of the house to his sprinkler control box and stopped abruptly.

The front cover of the box and its integrated combination lock had been smashed open as if hit head on by a sledgehammer. The dial timer and the control mechanisms, wires and plastic holders were in pieces and hung from the box lifelessly, dangling in mid-air.

Gruber lumbered around to the garage door, opened it with a combination on its keypad, went inside, turned off the water to the outside system and called the sprinkler company.

"Just plain and simple vandalism," the sprinkler service man told him two hours later. "I installed a new box. Glad we happened to have an opening, so I could get this fixed this afternoon. Given this incident, you might want to consider a motion detector camera for the property."

"It won't happen again," Gruber said emphatically. "Isn't this covered under our service contract or equipment warranty?" he demanded.

"No sir. The warranty on the box is long expired and

wouldn't cover this kind of thing anyway and it's not part of our service contract at all. You might try filing a claim with your home-owner's insurance, depending on your deductible. This is just one of those "shit happens" things," he shrugged. "Man, whoever did this sure nailed it, didn't they?"

"Young man, I deeply resent your impudence. This is a serious matter. I have called the police."

"Yes sir. Sorry about your trouble. Here is your invoice, Mr. Gruber."

"Well, god damn *you!*" Gruber erupted grabbing the invoice out of his hand.

He turned and at that unfortunate moment several boys, boys he did not recall seeing before, cruised by his house on their skateboards.

"Get away from my property!" he yelled at them waving the invoice in the air while the sprinkler repairman sidled over to his truck and drove off.

The kids looked at him strangely and picked up their pace.

The police came and with measured professionalism took his report while neighbors walked by noticing the police car and Gruber talking with them which made him even angrier.

After dinner at the Club, including several more martinis, Gruber slept badly. He dreamt that he was having a knock down drag out argument with his former wife, yet while they were screaming at each other he struggled to recall what it was they were fighting about. He dreamt that someone was tampering with his mail. He dreamt that his license plate with his personal initials had been removed from his SUV. Then he dreamt that the sprinkler system went off and ran for so long while he was asleep that his house drifted out and over the back yard and into Placid Lake, where it began to sink, trapping him in the bedroom.

He woke in the dark with a start and found himself drenched in sweat. He was out of breath and shaking with both fear and anger. Who could have done this? To HIM!

The time was 3:23am. He went into the bathroom and took a sleeping pill. He still slept badly and woke up late feeling disoriented, groggy and hung over. As he ate a breakfast of toast and coffee, he contemplated who could have vandalized his house.

There was that shifty Collier kid and his stupid teenage cohorts. They were probably the ones, or it could be an angered neighbor. That was possible, but who? He went through the long lists of recent infractions and letters he had had the management company write. The name, Merskey, kept surfacing on the edges of his consciousness and quickly he pushed it aside.

On his walk to the guard house he continued to feel a bit disoriented. Today everything seemed different somehow. Heavy humidity had crept in overnight and the air was hot and hazy, giving a slight distortion to his surroundings. He admonished himself. He needed to slow down on the martinis. Sleeping pills were not a great idea either. And the combination? Well, clearly he was feeling the effects.

He passed neighbors in the street that like the kids the day before he did not recognize, who looked at him like he was the one who was a stranger.

Cars that he did not recognize passed him. Some of the yards he walked by seemed to have changed ever so slightly, as if they had different landscaping, children's toys he had not seen before in driveways. Small disturbing things met his gaze at every turn.

He was relieved to find Herman at the guardhouse.

"Hey, Mr. G.!"

"Herman," he asked as they entered the guardhouse, "Did a number of new neighbors move in over the weekend?"

"No sir, well, at least no one on the weekend shift said anything about that."

"Ok... ask them, will you, when you get a chance?"

"Sure."

"Let's hear your report."

As they went through the daily infractions Herman had uncovered on his morning patrol, Gruber could not help but feel there was something different about him too. Finally, it dawned on him.

"Herman, are you growing a mustache?"

"Yes, Mr. G. Been at it awhile now, it's just beginning to fill in."

"Oh." He was pleased by this simple explanation.

As they were finishing up, a black limousine pulled up to the guard house and the driver's window rolled down.

When Herman opened the guardhouse door, the driver said, "Mr. Merskey would like a word with Mr. Gruber."

He pulled the car forward while Gruber came to the door. The tinted black rear window rolled down.

The small man in a white linen suit, black shirt and white silk tie, wearing dark wraparound sunglasses spoke to him from the cavernous air-conditioned interior.

"I hear you been havin' some trouble with your yhard."

"Yes sir," Gruber said in a tentative, puzzled tone.

"Sorry about that," Merskey said in his thin, gravelly voice, a small smile tugging at the corners of his mouth.

The tinted black window rolled closed slowly and the limousine pulled away down Sandhill Crane Drive.

After his session with Herman, Gruber walked hurriedly back to his house. Once there, he went to his gun cabinet, removed the shotgun he used for hunting game out to the east of their community, located shells, loaded the magazine and placed the shotgun in a corner, double checking that the safety was on.

He whiled away his time at lunch restlessly and abstractly, drinking only one martini, arrived back at his house and promptly fell into a deep sleep.

He awoke, checked the shotgun, showered and dressed for dinner.

The Club was busy that night. The new, fresh faced maitre d' was unaware of his customary table and after Gruber chewed him out, his waitress, whom he also did not recognize, timorously showed him to a table next to a crowd of residents he did not recognize raucously celebrating a 50th birthday and asked him for his club number.

"Young lady," he told her in a fury, "No one has asked me that in at least a decade."

"I'm sorry, sir. I'm new."

"Well, you may not be *for long*! Get me the manager!"

Gruber was pleased to see that he at least knew the manager, on whom he unloaded his customary tirade until sweat appeared on the manager's upper lip and he apologized profusely. And what did that get him? His table wasn't changed and he had to put up with the party next to him.

In his anger and frustration he ordered several

martinis, not even focusing on his dinner, until he finally weaved his way across the room and made his way into his Escalade and home where he fell into a restless and fitful sleep and woke much earlier than usual.

Walking rapidly to the guardhouse the next morning, not glancing to either side, he could smell the vague scent of juniper berries and vermouth emanating from his pores.

There was an interminable list of infractions for Herman and him to go through that morning. He responded distractedly and without any real interest as the time pushed on past noon.

As they were finishing, Merskey's limousine again pulled up to the guardhouse, this time stopping so that Merskey's window was in line with the door.

Gruber went out to the car.

The black tinted limousine window rolled down and Gruber was struck by the fact that Merskey seemed to be dressed exactly as he had been the day before.

"I have somethin' for you to think about," Merskey said, reaching out the window with a small, pale, wizened, claw like hand with beautifully manicured nails. It was if the hand was reaching out of a sarcophagus. He handed Gruber a white envelope.

The window glided back up and the limousine rolled away.

Gruber opened the envelope, trying unsuccessfully to steady his shaking hands as Herman looked over his shoulder.

"I'll be god damned," Gruber heard himself say, "It's a quotation."

"What's it say?"

Gruber read the typed quotation aloud, "Life is like a game, there could be many players. If you don't play with them, they'll play with you."

"Herman," he ordered, handing him the piece of paper, "Look that up on the computer. Who said that?"

"Ok, Mr. G.," Herman replied, a stressed tone in his voice.

He went to the computer, typed in the quotation, waited a moment and said, "Hitler."

"What?"

"It's a quote from Adolph Hitler," Herman said, trying without success to suppress a smile.

Gruber was struck by a terrible premonition. He vaulted from his chair.

He could not remember the last time that he ran. In attempting to, he realized in an instant that he no longer could. So, with a gait that was a cross between a walk, limp and a stagger he pushed his body as best he could, seeing himself as a pathetic and laughable figure, moving as fast as he could to his house. Soon in the heat and humidity his heart beat loudly in his chest. He felt nauseous. His gasps for air made strange, vibrating and wheezing noises. His hip joints screamed. A couple he did not recognize, walking their dachshund, stopped as he went by them and stared at him with alarm.

He arrived at his house in a state close to collapse, just in time to see water coursing from under his front and garage doors and to hear water cascading from inside his house and the avalanche sound of a ceiling crashing to the floor.

Gruber threw up his hands in horror and screamed in dismay at what he saw. He felt himself collapsing helplessly onto his lawn.

Out of his peripheral vision, he realized as he fell that a neighbor stood on the edge of his property, watching him.

He came down with a grunt into a seated position, smelling fresh cut grass and then a foul stench as his bowels erupted.

He looked at his house in disbelief and then over at his neighbor. "Please, help me!" he croaked.

It was a man he recognized, the tall, thin fellow with reddish hair and a lopsided face who ignored him whenever they might pass on their way around the community. He was the one whom Gruber had called Animal Control about twice because of his brindle pit bull bitch, now squatting at the end of her choke chain crapping on his lawn, looking at him with a joyful pit bull smile.

His neighbor did not respond to his plea, but merely watched him in his distress, a small cynical smile edging onto his features.

As the sounds of cascading water and collapsing ceilings continued throughout his house, Stanley Gruber heard himself sob.

VIII

Rebo

Here I am fully caffeinated, on a roll, making great headway on my research, trying to make a meaningful difference at the Institute and its continued policy relevance in the nation's capital, totally into it, when my boss, Joe Rebo, pokes his hang-dog face into my office and burbles in his avuncular manner, "Jenny. Got a minute?"

Through some congenital sinuses oddity his voice has a strange resonance to it, as if it's emerging from underwater. This idiosyncrasy adds to his sage and sometimes bemused persona.

I look up at him distractedly and try to mask my irritation. "Sure. Give me five."

By way of acknowledgement Rebo raises then lowers his heavy black eyebrows, runs a hand over his thick gunmetal hair then lifts his belt up on his paunch. "I'll go drain the radiator and see you in a bit."

"Gotcha," I say and sigh as he ambles down the hall. He's such a dinosaur. And I'm pissed. He's going to return, close the door to my cubicle, sit in the seat beside my door and babble, brilliant insights and critical information flashing like rare treasure amongst a truckload of garbage reflections as he takes a random mental drive down memory lane where it intersects the workaholic/ alcoholic highway.

Not only will I have to put up with his antique euphemisms but, even though I admire his savvy and unflappable demeanor, I am now going to have to endure being his sidekick which means I tack onto my workday as many hours as being a sidekick will take. Shit.

Our office, the fund raising, or development office, as we call it in the trade, is located on the third floor of the Institute's four-story building on K Street. Our floor houses different administration suites with one exception, the office of the former President of the United States. The former President has honored the Institute by accepting an appointment as a senior fellow. His office always makes me crack a smile when I pass it and glance in at the presidential seal and other regalia both presidential and personal that signify the presence of an eminence. The fact is that the former President shows up once or twice a year, usually for the National Policy Forum. In the meantime, his empty office is shown off regularly to visiting dignitaries and corporate officers as a feather in the Institute's cap. I have no idea what they pay the former President. On one hand, however much it is, it's probably worth it. On the other hand, such arrangements are one of several reasons the Institute's finances are reputedly in such serious difficulty, a fact known only by Institute's President, its CFO, Rebo and me, thanks to Rebo's martini enhanced lunches. Yes, despite all our wonderful progress as a society, there are still people who daily drink their lunch.

I turn in my chair and look out the window. Outside, it's a crisp spring day. The trees in their squares along the

sidewalk are just putting out new leaves, jonquils bloom-
ing in small bunches at their base and the atmosphere is
festive and crowded.

I notice that most people, instead of being absorbed in
their usual urgent march, are strolling aimlessly, enjoying the good weather. I make up my mind that I'm leaving the office on time for once, hightailing it back to my
apartment, taking my trail bike out, heading for the C&O
Canal towpath, on my way to Great Falls and some peace
and tranquility before darkness closes in. I eternally
thank my former boyfriend, Brad, for introducing me to
trail riding, at least before I figured out he was a two-tim-
ing, scumbag, dirtball.

At least Rebo didn't ask me to lunch. That would have
been two hours of martini enhanced chit chat and strat-
egizing, 'noodling,' as he would say. Not to mention that
there's this issue of this older guy accompanied by a young
woman. I mean, the looks we get sometimes when I'm in
his company. Not that they would care at the Dungeon,
his favorite place for lunch. It's such a friggin' dive but
sometimes, even there, folks walk in and just stare at us.
It's creepy. And Rebo loves the place. How he ever found
it and that such a place even exists in the nation's capital
is a mystery to me. Here we are in this elegant and sophis-
ticated city and where does Rebo choose to have lunch?
Milwaukee.

I mean to a certain degree it makes sense. Until three
years ago, Rebo spent his years at a Midwestern university, heading up their capital campaign, retiring when it
reached its goal of over $1 billion. He was not the kind to
ever consider permanent retirement and the idea of being
in the nation's capital and having a role of some import in

the making of policy, being in charge of bringing in all the fund-raising revenue, held some appeal. That and that the Institute was very much philosophically in tune with his work forever ethic made working here an easy choice, not to mention the fact that they threw a pile of money at him.

I am actually feeling a bit sorry for the guy. His wife died last year, multiple myeloma, a two-year battle, and so there's just a trace of sadness in everything he does. Plus, sometimes he acts like I'm his niece or something, or daughter, or God forbid, wife.

I feel myself shaking my head in disapproval of all of this, of the Institute, of Washington, DC, the world, life in general. Well, Rebo has forgotten more than I'll ever know and to know what's going down at the Institute it's mandatory that I hang out with him. Senatorial ethics: to get along, you go along.

I turn my attention back to my research. Three days ago an unsolicited gift of $100,000 arrived across the transom from a gentleman out West for the Institute's Agricultural Policy Program. As deputy director of fund raising, I smelled opportunity and volunteered to find out something about him.

What I found so far is very interesting. Through online research and calls to various contacts in federal agencies I discovered that the gentleman in question owns over a hundred and fifty thousand acres of farmland. Upon further inquiry it became apparent that he's receiving farm subsidies for not planting crops on much of his land. Okay, nothing out of the ordinary there. However, my next set of inquiries and even an examination of aerial views of the acreage revealed that significant portions of it are underwater. And for this same acreage this same individual is also receiving federal flood relief. I feel a small, cynical smile cross my face. This gives a new meaning to the phrase 'double dipping.' No wonder the interest in agriculture policy.

I now focus back on a wealth analysis screen that I had been retrieving when Rebo darkened my door and see quickly that our new prospect is a multi-billionaire, on the boards of two Fortune 500 companies and a number of local and national non-profits. He gives generously to them and to both political parties. What a great profile and what a wonderful person to include on the invitation list to our next annual National Policy Forum where CEO's, members of congress and the senate, government officials, embassy dignitaries, the Institute's scholars and fellows and even a few Hollywood types listen to presentations about the burning issues of the day and rub elbows. For anyone wishing to gain access, networks and insider knowledge, it is a 'can't miss' occasion. Access and influence, the two magical words powering any event in Washington, DC.

As I wrap up my analysis, I reflect that I will keep this research to myself until Rebo asks for it or until I can show it off to my advantage at a team meeting of the higher-ups.

As I save my files, Rebo walks in, closes the door behind him. He sits in the chair by my door.

"Sorry to be a little longer than I intended," he burbles, his eyebrows working up and down, "but I ran into our esteemed CFO in the Men's room...." Our esteemed CFO, Neil, is a wet behind the ears, balding peach fuzz nebbish who wears white short-sleeve dress shirts, ugly, cheap ties, grey Dockers that are an inch too short, worn out cotton socks and unpolished black wingtips, who I can tell wants to ask me out but, thankfully, doesn't have the first clue on how to do it. Rebo knows all this, or intuits it, and his 'esteemed' characterization is his way of making a little joke.

"You know where I'm headed next?"

"Haven't a clue."

"Meeting with the president, the board chair and several of the more well-heeled board members about the upcoming capital campaign. We're going to show them renderings of the new Institute headquarters.... Like to see them?"

"Sure."

Rebo stands, lifts his pants up onto his paunch and heads off into his office. He returns a few moments later with a set of large rolled up renderings.

He closes my door and unrolls a first rendering against it. It shows an attractive, glossy rendition of a very prosperous looking office building. It almost has a resort look to it with a lovely colonnade terrace on the top level.

"This is...?" I ask just to be sure.

"Our new headquarters."

"Damn, Rebo. It's awesome."

"The plan is to buy and renovate the building, use the top two floors for the Institute. We'll have our own dining room, conference center, all the trappings, and to rent out the other floors to tenants which helps amortize our annual expense, may even make money. Also allows us to expand if need be as leases are up.

"Where is it going to be located?"

"I'm sworn to secrecy on that, but I can tell you that those two upper floors would have a view of the Treasury building and the White House."

"Wow."

He went through the rest of the renderings which detailed the interior of the building, looking out over the Treasury with the White House in the background. Utterly knockout impressive.

"How much is all this going to cost?"

Rebo's eyebrows went up and down, his jowls shaking a little, while he considered the question. "Around $60 million. Of course, we'll want to have a parallel effort to raise funds for endowment and for enhancement funds for different programs."

He put the set of rolled up renderings aside between the chair and credenza along my wall and sat down looking a bit glum.

"Is something wrong?"

"So, Jenny, in the Men's room Neil told me that if we don't raise $500,000 by Friday he can't meet payroll."

"What? Rebo, it's fucking Wednesday."

"I'm aware of that."

"Has he completely lost it?"

"'Fraid not, although his bowels may have lost it.... There's something I haven't told you."

"Yeah?"

"He told me the same thing last month."

"But we made payroll, right?"

"Yes we did."

"How?"

He smiled, bemused. "It's the damnedest thing. I came in the following Monday and as soon as they brought around my paycheck I hurried down the alley beside us to the Dumbarton Bank and Trust and cashed it."

He smiled sheepishly. "I'm sorry I didn't say anything to you but I really wasn't sure what the hell was going on. In any case, nothing happened. The Institute just kept on running, no one saying word or acting at all like there was any problem.

"So, that following Wednesday, I went over to Finance, walked into Neil's office, shut the door and asked the young man just what the hell was going on.

"He's obviously got no one else to talk to but me and no one upstairs is telling him anything. He's scared to death. He unloaded his troubles.... Seems that last month over the weekend before payroll there was an anonymous wire transfer of $500,000 made to our accounts."

"Anonymous?"

"From the Middle East."

"Holy shit."

"That's what I said, except with a couple more expletives. As you're undoubtedly aware, money flows in strange ways and from strange places these days, some of it clandestine. Hard to know in fact where the hell this money came from. Obviously, our president knows and he has many friends in high places both here and abroad. There's someone or some entity out there that wants to assure the Institute's survival. So, now Neil's telling me we're short $500,000 again."

"Rebo, this is serious. We don't want to know anything more about this."

"Oh, I agree, but Neil kept on talking. It gets worse."

"Worse?"

He looked at me directly. "The Institute is up to its asshole in debt. They've collateralized everything for a line of credit to bring on more important big names as scholars and fellows in the calculated risk that this increased prominence will bring in more bucks in fund raising and contracts. The line of credit is coming due. That's part of what's got Neil scared shitless."

"Jesus."

"It gets worse still."

"Worse? How could it get worse still?"

"The president instructed Neil to create two sets of books, one detailing the different endowments created by our individual, corporate and foundation donors, the annual investment return of those accounts, their payout to the operating budget and their new annualized totals. Neil's done that and sent quarterly reports to each endowment donor."

"Ohhhh-kay. So that's standard operating procedure. What's wrong with that?"

"Our president has spent the endowment. The reports Neil sent out are fictitious."

"Spent it! All of it! That's millions and millions of dollars! By board by-laws, by all the ethical standards governing non-profits, endowments are to be held and invested with a set yearly payout."

"He's also instructed Neil to create a second set of books that details our actual budget, expenditures, cash flow etc. sans endowment so they can keep an accurate track of our actual financials."

"That's theft! That's fraud! Some of the endowment donors are Fortune 500 companies. What the hell is he thinking?" I hear my voice tinged with horror.

Rebo looked out the window behind me for moment, 'noodling', and then focused on me again, burbled, "Yep."

"What'd he spend it on?" I could hear the horrified disbelieving tone in my voice.

"For starters, architectural fees, these renderings I just showed you, some earnest money to get an option on this new building, initial deposit to the developer, signing bonuses to some new scholars and fellows who needed a little persuasion to join us. Who knows what else. I don't get the sense that any of it was personal, just leveraging."

I was flummoxed. "He thinks he's going to get away with this? He thinks we're going to build this great Taj Mahal new headquarters when we can't even make payroll?"

"Yeah, actually he does. He figures the upcoming campaign will raise so much money that he'll just replace what he's referring to as 'internal borrowing' and everything will just turn out hunky dory."

"And you're going along with this?"

Rebo considered my question. "You know, Jenny, you have to look at the long haul here. The gentlemen and lady board members we're meeting with upstairs today have an estimated gift capacity of over $25 million. Properly motivated they could solve our little issues here in the snap of fingers.

"So, to that end I'm going up to my meeting with the bigwigs. You do your best to see whether you can rein in any prospective gifts from our most stalwart supporters, particularly the corporations. Call 'em up, ask them where we are in their pipeline of consideration. If a gift is about to be forthcoming, you might try suggesting a wire transfer as a seamless way to do business. Tell them a number of our other donors are choosing to do things that way these days. They might actually buy that. Let's also hope there's another little love offering from overseas over the weekend." He paused.

I looked at him for a long moment. "Okay, boss."

Rebo picked up the renderings, opened the door and walked into his office to grab his suit jacket.

Then I watched him amble down our suite toward the former President's office and the elevator, my phone call to the executive recruiter I'd flirted with at the last conference already ringing.

IX

Henry

I did not want to go. Audrey talked me into it. She thought it would 'interesting' to accept Henry's invitation to dinner at their place. 'Interesting' as in being a morbidly curious spectator at a car wreck. Sometimes I wonder about Audrey. But then again, Henry's going through tough times. Perhaps I can cheer him up.

He is, after all, my best friend. We grew up together in the Washington, DC suburbs and still live here. As we drive to their house, I daydream. We are kids again, standing, facing each other, a couple feet apart and he is like he was then – smart and funny and clever and full of himself, a big mop of hair over an angelic face with a special, mischievous grin that he showed only to friends. All the teachers and girls were snowed and he did not really care except that it was fun pulling cons on them and doing whatever the hell he pleased. I could just feel him like that, his presence. We were back to our old partnership, two schemers hatching great plans to upend the entire universe, i.e. grade school.

We pull into the circular driveway of Henry and Pamela's place, a 9,500 square foot colossus of intricately melded architectural motifs -- Georgian first floor, Gothic second with a turret, Tudor garage, Spanish great room, asphalt driveway, a heavily varnished front door with over-sized, brass plate colonial sconces on each side.

Pamela is her usual showy, saccharine and arsenic self. She and Audrey act as if they cannot not be more excited to see one another, while I stand by and watch with amazement. Ordinarily I might have watched in admiration, knowing Audrey is putting on a good show to help preserve my relationship with Henry, but there is more to it than that. Henry and Pamela are widely viewed to be on their way out as a couple; as well, Pamela is an incorrigible gossip. Yes, interesting.

What is it with our friends anyway? All the wonderful people we had met in our younger years, with whom we had spent countless hours at the beach, lake and pool parties, ski trips, sports and league events and at each other's houses now seemed to be caught up in a collective catastrophe of divorce, disease, drugs or malfeasance, in several cases all of the above.

I beat a hasty retreat to the back yard where Pamela tells me with more than a little disdain that Henry is engaged in some form of barbecue insanity.

On my way I flashback on Pamela in the early days, in cut-off's and a t-shirt, as we tubed down the sleepy, mid-summer Shenandoah passing a wine bottle between us. Nature's child is now a different woman entirely.

Forty degrees of dark and increasingly windy late October chill and Henry is at the propane-powered brick spit, the centerpiece of the world's largest patio, designed in such a way that one wonders whether methamphetamine was involved.

A brick wall undulates around us, a brick bench seat

in each undulation with a wrought iron cup holder and a wrought iron tray table on a hinge. The huge gas-powered spit glows in the dark. Henry is in his usual semi-disheveled state, everything a bit overgrown – hair, chin, stomach, a flaccid guy in designer sweats and leather coat.

"Hey, man!" he half shouts at me, waving, "You're a sight for sore eyes! Some Jack?" He motions at the Jack Daniels bottle on the brick table beside him.

"Sure.... Henry, what the hell have you done here?"

I pick up the empty can of lighter fluid laying on the brick table. "It's not like you need this, you know. You just turn on the gas."

"You should have been here a few minutes ago when I lit this conflagration. Big explosion."

I shake my head. "Always looking for a new high, huh?"

Henry looks at me. "No. Truthfully, trying to ward off the cold and burn off some depression. And you know what?"

"What?"

He smiles a crooked smile. "It kind of worked."

I sigh and take a swig from the bottle. "Man, I hate seeing you like this."

"Ahhh, don't feel so bad," he says as he throws minute steaks, hamburgers and hot dogs onto different sections of the grill.

Five years ago Henry and his company pioneered an encryption system for HMO's and medical centers to assure their records' security. Three years ago he sold the company for several hundred million. Since then he has dabbled in venture capital projects, partnerships, real estate and, thankfully, the stock market, all of which have made money, facts of which I am keenly aware because

I am Henry's broker. Perhaps another reason Audrey thought it would make sense for us to be here.

So what is it about best friends in general and Henry in particular? Are we condemned by destiny to be inextricably linked for life or is it like Audrey is fond of saying – that every friendship has a shelf life that at one point or another through no fault of either party will expire? I think about this while Henry and I have a couple more swigs of bourbon and he finishes with the barbecuing.

He scoops the last of the steaks and hamburgers and hot dogs onto a large platter.

He turns to me and sighs, "Do we have to go back inside?"

"Yeah, but we could come back out here after dinner."

"Small consolation."

"Yeah."

"I think I need a tree house like we had when we were kids, except an adult tree house. You know, with a small space heater and a little insulation, an extension cord, a case of Dinty Moore beef stew, a mini-bar, an occasional trip to the pool house for life's necessities."

"Sounds idyllic."

"Ah, yes, my boy... by comparison, by comparison... it would be."

The French doors open with a shudder into a blaze of light and heat from their massive, wall-to-wall carpeted family room with leather furniture and a home theatre.

"We'll be having dinner in the dining room, I suppose," Henry says. He shrugs. "If you're not into steaks or burgers, Pamela ordered some Thai and Chinese. The cook quit, so most nights it's carry out for dinner. That's why you build a hundred-thousand-dollar gourmet kitchen."

Pamela is wearing caramel colored leather pants with a gold metal belt, a close fitting, ribbed, white turtleneck, a multi-colored silk scarf, brassy earrings, spike heels.

Their Pomeranian, Sasha, screeches behind her, pawing at her leg for attention. She picks the dog up and nuzzles it.

"Does Daddy upset you, lover dog?"

She looks at Henry with disapproval.

The dog yaps confirmation.

"Amazing what obedience school can accomplish," Henry comments to no one in particular. "Oh, Honey, I wasn't talking to you. Obviously you haven't been."

"I can see this is going to be a fun evening," I say to both of them. "Very adult."

Their domestic, Simon, appears, a strong but neutral presence, Australian. "The table is ready."

I have never really become accustomed to Henry and Pamela having servants, although in their case, Simon seems to help because he neutralizes the squabbling.

The dining room table has been set with Martha Stewart china and flatware.

Henry sets the platter of steak, hamburgers and hot dogs on a heat proof mat at the table's center, next to containers of oriental food.

"Dinner!" he bellows.

The children enter. Henry Jr., a slight, brown haired boy with an anxious, nearsighted squint, is dressed in the giant clothes worn by every fourteen-year-old with a different touch in the large ersatz diamond in a pierced left ear lobe.

"Shades of the NBA," Henry says, noticing my stare.

"Can you dunk, yet?" I ask, feeling like a stupid adult the moment I say it.

"Naw," Henry Jr. replies. "I gotta grow some."

"Soon enough.... You play on a team?"

"Naw."

"He couldn't make the JV this year, so he'll try again next year," Pamela informs me. "And you haven't said hello to little Elizabeth."

Elizabeth is a chubby little girl with a pixie haircut and the nice smile affected by little girls who have been told that they are perfect to the point they believe it.

Elizabeth is dressed in a pink crinoline Sugar Plum Fairy costume.

"My little ballerina," coos Pamela. "We're trying out for the ballet's "Nutcracker" next week. Isn't that exciting!?" she says to Elizabeth.

"Mommy says," Elizabeth parrots in a high, singsong voice, "It is a very difficult competition, but wouldn't it be wonderful if I would be chosen!"

At dinner Simon disappears while we pass around the plates and the paper containers.

Henry eats large, multiple portions of Thai and Chinese voraciously, sullen, disconsolate, looking none of us in the eye, saying not a word.

"So, where are you in school?" I ask Henry, Jr. I feel that I should pay some attention to him because he is my godchild, even though I sense any attention paid to him is badly regarded by Pamela.

"He's at Pyle," Pamela answers, "okay for him. Lizzy's doing very well at Sidwell. Senator Promeus's daughter and Secretary Wright's son are in her class."

"Great."

Audrey asks, "Tell us about your school play, Lizzy, that your Mom told me you are in?"

Lizzy rocks back and forth and tells us, her hands clasped before her, rotating this way and that.

"The play we are doing is called *Godspell* and it was originally written and performed in the 1970's and it's really weird but nice, kind of just like people were back then – you know everybody believed in peace and love, not like today."

Henry looks up for a moment, looks at me, raises his eyebrows.

"Pamela was telling me about her involvement in Metro Women," Audrey informs me.

Prompted by Audrey's comment, Pamela eagerly adds, "It is such a fine group of leading Washington area women. I'm honored to be included," she says with unconvincing humility. "Every Wednesday we have a luncheon speaker. Like last week it was Cookie Claymore, the television anchor, who talked with us about the opioid babies at Armory General and how we could help by adopting or identifying families who might. You know what's fascinating is that most of the babies are adopted by hospital workers. They stop by during work hours to help take care of these infants and end up becoming attached to them. Metro Women keeps us informed about contemporary issues. The money raised from our events, like our fashion show and our polo party, goes directly to charities."

"Can I be excused?" Henry Jr. asks plaintively. He has taken a hamburger but has eaten little of it.

"Yes, dear."

When he has left, Pamela says, "I don't know what it

is we did, but that kid just doesn't have it. We've tried everything – tutors, summer camp, but you can only do so much when they're dim."

"It could be worse," Henry remarks, "he could've inherited your disposition."

"Don't be such a wiseass, or I'll..."

Simon appears to begin clearing the table, causing Pamela to halt any further remarks.

"I want a cup of coffee," she demands of Simon in a recriminating tone, "and this time it better not be bitter like last time."

"Yes madam," Simon says flatly, calmly.

Henry rises. "May I be excused?" he asks imitating Henry Jr.'s plaintive tone.

The French doors shiver and quake and cold air rushes in over the dry heat of the indoors. Henry and I make our way out to the grill, each of us holding a go-cup of liberally poured bourbon. The grill flames away unnaturally but gives out welcome heat.

As we sip our bourbon, I think about a few months before when Audrey and I had attended a memorial for a former boss of mine, an avuncular man with a great mind, admirable knowledge and experience whose daily consumption of alcohol, cigarettes and bad food had assured his early demise. The service was held in the Cathedral neighborhood in the elegant social room of an antique apartment building where he had lived.

My boss's best friend stood up and spoke with difficulty but also with eloquence of shared, time distant adventures – sunsets in different foreign lands, crashing sailboats into piers, meeting wives and friends, career accomplishments, pride in the profession. I had met this friend for a few, fleeting moments previously, simply knowing him as someone with whom my boss had surreptitious drinks on Friday afternoons. His eulogy brought out whole different dimensions of someone I thought I knew quite well and left not a dry eye in the house.

Was this how Henry and I would end up? One of us eulogizing the other?

Henry gazes at the flames. "Sorry..." he says, shrugging. "It was a bad idea inviting you guys out here. I just thought... you know, old friends... old times." He shrugs again. "You know she wasn't always this way.... It's the money. Ruined her; going to ruin the kids."

"Stop feeling sorry for yourself. We're both glad to see you and I can't say Pamela isn't kind of fascinating in a horror film kind of way. I am somewhat curious about what you intend to do to resolve things. Somehow I find it hard to believe that Pamela's going to be that cooperative."

Henry looks at me. Slowly he smiles, "She hasn't been a very good girl of late. For starters, a peccadillo with her personal trainer, a lovely fellow named Guido."

"Oh."

"It's tacky, but that's why you hand over such matters to rodent PI's and lawyers. Right now I'm simply kind of in mourning. I suspect it will pass. As for the divorce, it's already negotiated; the papers are signed. We're just waiting for our day in court. She agrees to my terms. She'll be supported nicely by a trust for the rest of her life. No exposure of her misdeeds forthcoming.... I maintain custody; she has visitation rights. She gets to run her own foundation, which will allow her leverage in the game of 'Ultimate Pretension.'

"This house, I hate this house, is going to be gone in

a nanosecond. Already have some other actual homes lined up to look at. I think I'll keep Simon around. He's a rock. In a weird way, I'm looking forward to being a single parent, with a nanny of course. But I'll be attending PTA, helping with homework, driving them around. Don't you think I'll be an ideal Dad?"

"Uhhhh..."

Henry laughs, "When I talk about this stuff all of a sudden I feel like I'm beginning to be alive again. It's great to know I still have you and Audrey as friends. Look, if there's anything I can do for you, Audrey and the kids, don't hesitate to ask. Okay?"

"Thanks for the offer but having you as a friend is enough."

Henry steps toward me and offers his hand and smiling like idiots we both spontaneously give one another the secret handshake of our youth. It brings back grade school antics, forts in the woods, sneaking out at night and roaming our neighborhoods looking for trouble.

"When was the last time we did that?" he asks.

"I have no idea."

"Friends for life," he smiles.

"It's true," I say. I am feeling increasingly ill at ease.

I sigh, "I guess we better get going."

"Sure."

X

Site Visit

The inner city. A hot, humid Saturday summer day. "This must be it," I told Evan as I glanced at the GPS.

To our right was a long, one-story, rundown concrete block building, its exterior darkened by years of dirt and pollution, its medium blue paint peeling, exposing the block underneath, a few small windows covered with black security grating. Derelict was the word that came to mind.

I parked. The curb and sidewalk were broken up, weeds growing in cracks and crevices, a few shards of broken glass from liquor bottles scattered here and there. Opening my door, I was greeted by the smell of hot asphalt, baking concrete and urine.

A tall, rail thin man in a tan/yellow hued suit, clerical shirt and collar, shaved head and a straw hat with a tan and yellow rep band was walking toward us, obviously on his way to our same destination.

He saw us, flashed us a look of recognition and changed course to meet us. "Gentlemen," he said as he approached, "Let me introduce myself. I presume you're the campaign consultants I've been hearing good things about, the guys that'll raise the money to get us a new Youth Transition

Center for the Harbor Home Society. Lord knows we need it. I'm the Reverend Samuel Cornelius, or Reverend Sam as the kids call me, the center's part time director."

We shook hands. "Jeff Peters," I told him, "And my associate, Evan Smith."

"This building here, Jeff and Evan," Reverend Sam said, gesturing at it, "It's a former motel, more like a flop house. It don't look like much, because it isn't, but it has one attribute. The owner is letting us use it rent free. We had a team come in and completely stripped and cleaned the place. That being said, as you'll discover, sometimes with free you get what you pay for, but to these foster young men and women for at least now, this is their home and they're fixing it up. I been buyin' whatever they need, particularly paint, masking tape, ladders, what all. You'll see what I'm talking about. They're stoked about having their own place." He smiled at the thought of their enthusiasm.

A car door slammed behind us and, turning, we saw that the campaign co-chairs had arrived together in a black Impala being driven by Herman Hargrove. Herman was the founder, chairman and CEO of Nomis Technology. With the success of his rapidly growing regional company he was now a refined geek, thin and wiry with yellow-tinted designer glasses, expensive casual Friday clothes and a big Rolex. The other co-chair, the formidable Ms. Melvin, the founder of Maureen Melvin Executive Search, was in a tailored blue business suit and ruffled blouse.

As they walked toward us, from the traffic light intersection a block away a rapid honking sounded. A large container truck ran the light and made a left turn onto the street. Continuing its honking as a warning to people on the sidewalks, the truck made a sweeping turn onto the left sidewalk and came around until it stopped, straddling both lanes, its cab now on the right sidewalk.

"Uh-oh," Reverend Sam said, "Folks, we didn't arrange this. It's no demonstration."

"What's going down?" Herman asked. His voice was a pleasant baritone, not what you would expect from his physique.

"That's a drug house down there. I believe what we're looking at is a raid. You can see why it's not good for kids in this neighborhood."

The tailgate door of the truck rolled up with a large noise. Armored police jumped out and pulled out the loading ramp which crashed down. More armored police streamed down the ramp, those in the lead carrying a ram. They ran up the stairs to the rowhouse and crashed through its door. Gun shots sounded and we saw people on the street start running.

"Uh, we should definitely get inside," Reverend Sam said.

"Does this happen often?" Ms. Melvin asked plaintively as we hustled to the doorway.

"Every couple months or so. Soon as the police leave all the dealing comes back."

We entered the main entrance through a blue painted steel door. Once we were inside, Reverend Sam slammed it shut and pulled down a bar latch from the side, locking us in the building.

On the street we could hear shouting which became louder, closer to us. Then we heard people running by the building. Several shots sounded, close by. I glanced at Evan. He looked scared.

"Don't anyone be worried," the Reverend Sam said to us. "Anyone around here knows who we are, who the kids are. They leave us alone."

There was a momentary silence. I wondered what the hell we were doing there, what trouble I might have made for Evan and me. New accounts were always a puzzle for us to solve. So far, this was the first account where the prospect of being shot at was a distinct possibility. A new challenge that would not be shared with one's wife and children.

Of course, our selection had been through a competing bid process, which involved our usual expression of enthusiasm for the cause while wondering just what we might be getting ourselves into.

The reasons for our being selected were relatively simple yet relatively complicated. Simple because we had worked previously with Herman in his role as co-chair of a capital renovation campaign for the downtown YMCA. He had had his doubts about us until I had scripted his and the Y's president's visit to a national foundation on behalf of a million-dollar challenge grant. They had hit a home run. Herman had called me from their taxi immediately after the meeting and asked, "Jeff, how the HELL did you do that?"

"Do what?"

"They asked exactly what you said they would ask, word for damned word. We had the right answers sitting right in front of us in our open portfolios. Slam dunk, my friend. You're a magician."

Well, I had been to that same foundation three or four times before, so I knew the drill. The problem, however, for this campaign was that it would be far more difficult than the YMCA's. For starters no one knew about Harbor. It was an unknown organization for the forgotten, foster children and youth.

The complicated part of our selection was Ms. Melvin. There was a natural inclination among many to suspect professional fund raisers to be slick, two-faced, shiny shoed crooks, looking to somehow cheat them out of their hard-earned grant money, that every word that passed through our lips was an ulterior manipulative lie. And the fact was that some in our profession fit this description to a T. The level of trust granted our profession as measured by numerous surveys was only one or two percentage points above that of congress. Not exactly a reassuring statistic.

We often spent a lot of time at the front end of accounts trying to establish trust and then the rest of our tenure trying to establish the confidence required for success. So, Ms. Melvin clearly had her doubts and had set about asking behind the scene, unacknowledged questions about our capabilities.

How did I know this? Her questions were written indelibly all over her face, her expression in our presence changing from doubtful to baleful to contemptuous flashing different colors of attitude like a neon sign on a moonless night. Her interview questions had followed suit. Questions that were fine, our credentials, our inner-city experience, similar campaigns, morphed into questions that gave us pause, did we have children, where did we live, when did Evan graduate from college, did we work well with strong A-Type women? That a crack executive recruiter was breaking best practice protocol rules for an interview told me something about how emotionally involved she was in the cause. A mama bear protecting her cubs.

In the final analysis the fact that Evan had conducted our work for the YMCA and would be managing their campaign had likely been the deciding factor. Evan was meticulous and had a unique capability of mirroring the interests and attitudes of those with whom he worked, so he was able to get along with virtually everyone while still maintaining a steady hand on forward momentum.

"Well," Reverend Sam said, "Let's meet some of these young men and women. Malcolm's over here in the education center. He'll come along with us."

Malcolm was Harbor Home's executive director. We liked Malcolm, with whom we already had several briefing meetings. His enthusiasm and deep commitment to the organization and its cause was great asset, immediately excusing his corpulence.

For the first time I looked around. We were standing in what had formerly been the reception area which led to a hallway with low ceiling tiles and old dry wall. The place smelled of Lysol. The floor was black and white linoleum tiles worn through in places and darkened from use.

We walked down the hall to a former conference room that had been converted into a dining hall/classroom education center, rows of metal folding tables and chairs in straight lines facing the front of the room where a table sat with a projector, a portable screen set up at the front wall, a table to the side with refreshments, the recently carpeted floor giving off an unpleasant smell.

Malcolm met us at the doorway. Obviously motivated

by his perceived importance of our meeting, he had dressed in an olive-green summer suit that must have been a challenge to put on. He was being strangled by a purple tie and was sweating profusely, had already pitted out his suit.

"Another raid?" he asked Sam.

"Yeah, same ol', same ol'."

"Okay," Malcolm said with a tinge of regret. He turned his attention to us. "Welcome everyone!" he said, clasping his hands together. "I thought we would start with a tour of this current facility. It speaks eloquently of our needs."

Herman spoke up. "On one condition. Get rid of that damned suit jacket."

We laughed which helped break the tension we were still feeling from the street.

Malcolm left his jacket on the chair inside the education center, unbuttoned his top button, loosened his tie and we walked down the hall to another blue painted steel door.

"We're about to enter what we're calling our dormitory," Malcolm told us. "Each youth has his or her own room. They have to be in bed by 11 pm. We have a nightly hall proctor, a former cop, to assure there are no visitors or goings on between rooms. I'm proud of this group. Twelve of 'em. Five are going to community college, four have jobs, the rest are trying like hell. No pregnancies. Right now, they're about the business of fixing up the place."

He pulled the steel door open. The smell of paint was almost overwhelming.

In the narrow light green, bright florescent lit hallway, lined alternately by room doors, in the midst of whoops and giggles a paint fight was going on among five residents. They were spattering one another with paint from their brushes, at least for the instant before they recognized our presence. In the next instant they stood frozen with guilt-ridden expressions.

A tall young man walked toward us, a big streak of yellow paint running down his cheek and neck and across his sweatshirt. He said to Malcolm and Reverend Sam, "Sorry guys, we got a little out of hand. But don't worry it's water based. We'll clean it up."

"Ok, Tommie," Reverend Sam said, "That clean up could begin about now, don't you think?"

"Oh, sure..."

"But first," Malcolm interjected, "Let me make some introductions to our guests."

"Tommie Hampton here is training at the community college to be a lab technician."

"Yeah," Tommie told us, "I'm in my first year. Had to get a GED first. Transition Center helped me do that."

"Hey," another youth spoke up, a young man who could most accurately be described as a white Rastafarian with ginger colored frizz in dreadlocks and ample amateur body art on his arms, hands and neck, the kind applied in jail, "I know who Mr. Hargrove is and Ms. Melvin is. They come an' mentor us and stuff but who these people?"

"They're our guests, Willie," Malcolm told him evenly.

"Wha' youall doin' here?"

"They're professional fund raisers, Willie, going to help us raise the money for our new center."

"Fun raisers? You mean like hell raisers? That'd be gud. Hell, no one wanna give us any mon-ney. No one care 'bout us. Never have, never will. You ain't gonna raise any mon-ney for us. You jus' gonna take it. That's the rule. Take whatever you can get offa us. Doun give no shit. I tell you what. I bet you my in-tire lif' savins'," he paused for effect, "Forty-three dollar and eighty-five cent that you don' raise 'nuf mon-ney. Wanna bet?"

"I'll take that bet," Herman announced. He stepped toward Willie and they shook hands, Willie glaring at us defiantly.

"Okay," Malcolm said, trying to get our visit back on track, "Our guests here would like to see one of your all's rooms. Someone whose room might be presentable."

A young lady in pig tails at the back spoke up, "Mahn's presentable. I painted it PURPLE!"

"Okay," Malcolm said to us, "Let's take a look. Let me introduce you to Melanie Montgomery who's studying early childhood education."

We made our way down the hall to her room. It was a small, windowless rectangle, with a single bed, made up with a blanket and sheet, a small second-hand rickety desk with a laptop on it and a small bookshelf in which school books lay, a tiny folding metal door closet on one side next to a worn second-hand bureau. The room was indeed purple, the floor the same worn linoleum as in the hallway but it was meticulously clean and its new paint had been applied with great care.

"Very nice, Melanie," Ms. Melvin said. "You did a nice job."

"Thank you, Ms. Melvin. I 'preciate that."

"Okay," Malcolm said. I knew he was anxious to get on with his presentation. "Let's get back to the education center."

After we had served ourselves some coffee and other

refreshments, we took seats at different tables, Malcolm stood in front of the room and spoke to us. His presentation was mostly for our benefit but also to bring us together.

"First of all, let me apologize for Willie acting out. He needs a job, but he also needs to change his behavior. Not easy. Gives you just a brief idea of the challenges these youth face. I fear for Willie. Now I know most of you know at least some of this, but the sad fact is that our state, when these kids reach the age of eighteen, drops any support for them. They've grown up without families in a system that has housed them in foster homes or with temporary foster families, some who care and others who are just in it for the money. Many have suffered abuse in their real families and have nowhere to turn, no relative or family friends who would take them in. Some are suffering from post-traumatic stress syndrome from being beaten or raped. They've not been adopted into a forever home. Their education has been spotty at best. They've lived a life of dependence. So, on their eighteenth birthday, our state in effect says, 'Happy birthday. You're homeless.'

"That's where we come in. Here in this room we offer them counseling on the real world and how to deal with their deficit of life skills. We coach the young men and women starting at square one on the basics of how to apply for, interview for a job, how to open, use and balance a bank account, how to buy groceries and other things they might need. I gotta thank Ms. Melvin for her help with these kids. She teaches a class here and works with the individual youth and in some cases has even found them internships and employment. Herman has helped counsel them on their setting education and employment goals. We work with a host of other volunteers on helping them fill out applications for all the real world help they can get from job or community college applications to Medicaid. You name it.

"The facts are that without this center that we're in today, the twelve kids here some who you've barely met, at age eighteen 20% would have been instantly homeless with more to follow, 7 out of 10 girls would become pregnant before the age of twenty-one, less than 3% would ever earn a college degree, only 1 out of 2 would have a real job with a salary and benefits before they are twenty-four.

"Now you see the conditions these young people are in presently, yet they are working hard through our education and training programs to make a success of their lives. Think of all we could accomplish with the new Youth Transition Center, which could house double or triple the number of residents. Think of the cost to society of a life of dependence if we don't do something to break this cycle through building this new facility. Now I'll get off my pulpit and let me show you some features of our new center."

While Malcolm went through his slides which featured a beautiful rendering of the new Youth Transition Center and continued on to its well thought out interior space and the expanded education and job training programs, I reflected on the challenge of raising $5 million for the building and its programming.

The good news was that a local developer who had been adopted as a child had contributed five acres of land near the city limits, near a partner public high school and within a few miles of the community college, so we had signature lead gift that gave credibility and hope to the project. Herman had ponied up a half-million and Ms. Melvin two hundred and fifty thousand. So, we were off to a good start. We had a short list of prospective honorary chairs who would bring regional recognition and importance to the campaign and who might help with additional lead gifts. We had identified local, regional and national prospects. A trailer to house the campaign was being set up along the side of the construction trailer on the new site. A great deal of effort would be expended over the next two years.

Malcolm ended his presentation, thanking us for being there and as we all rose to leave, he said to me and Evan, "Hey, can you guys stick around for a minute."

"Sure."

We walked with Reverend Sam, Herman and Ms. Melvin to the entrance. Reverend Sam swung back the bar on the door, opened it and took a precautionary look outside.

"Uh, all clear. Except one thing. Herman, your car's been hit."

We walked out with them and sure enough there was a bullet hole in the left side of the Impala's front windshield, crazed safety glass surrounding it, right where the passenger would normally sit. I was sure there would be collateral damage inside.

"Hey," Herman chuckled, "No worries, folks. It's a rental. No way I'm bringin' the Mercedes down here. Maureen, probably a good idea for you to sit in the back seat. I'll be the chauffeur. Drivin' Ms. Melvin. They can make a movie of us."

Ms. Melvin found no amusement in Herman's

comment, but when they reached the car she did get into the back seat behind him.

As they drove off, Reverend Sam turned to us and said, "Pleasure to meet you gentlemen. I'll be on my way."

We shook hands.

Back in the conference room we sat at one of the metal tables. Malcolm put his fingers tips together, looked at me, then looked at Evan. "I'm relieving Reverend Sam of his duties," he told us.

"Oh..." I heard myself say.

"He's been skimming the monthly youth transition education program grant funding. Has himself a nice new, leased BMW."

"Stealing from these kids?" Evan said, much more loudly than I'm sure he intended.

"Did he know this when we met today?" I asked.

"Oh yeah. Fucking two-faced bastard. I confronted Sam about it and then called the BMW dealer and told him what was going on and that the Reverend would need to return the car. Instead of being a cold-hearted mother, he refunded Sam's lease down payment and took the car back and tore up the lease. Thank God. Ms. Melvin has offered to do a *gratis* search for his replacement. I'll keep him involved as a volunteer. The kids like him and he brings some value as a man of the cloth. Sam can jus' go on skimming from his congregation but not from us."

"Wow."

"Ms. Melvin wants someone more empathetic, read motherly, who can be both a role model and a mentor to these kids. I'm not sure how she'll pull that off. We'll see."

We sat there, looking at one another.

Evan said, "What are we going to do about Willie?"

Malcolm and I looked at him, surprised.

"What do you mean?" Malcolm asked.

"He needs some help. What could we do to help him?"

"We meaning?"

"Us individually. Maybe our company." He looked at me.

Malcolm looked at me.

"Sure," I said, "I'm for that. I can talk to our partners."

"Willie's trying to find work as a carpenter's apprentice. It's something he's good at and interested in. Maybe you guys could provide some upfront funding for that. Make him a whole lot more acceptable to folks in the trade. In fact, there's this project being run by a local non-profit here, big grant from a major U.S. corporation where they're using at risk youth to help renovate housing in some neighborhoods around here. Basically, these young men and women are learning employable job skills renovating their own neighborhoods. Terrific program. I could call the executive director and see whether they might be interested in taking on an additional person."

"Okay," I told him, "We'll get back to you. If I can't get our partners to go along, Evan and I will figure out what we can do personally and what other sources we might access."

"Ok, man. That would be great." I could see Malcolm was both touched and pleased by our initiative.

"Sure," I said and felt myself smiling. I looked over at Evan who was grinning.

I stood and held out my hand. Malcolm reached out and took it with a firm grasp and then taking a step forward gave me a brief one-armed hug. "Thank you," he said. "We're a team then."

"Right," I told him and watched Evan nodding.

In the car on the way out of the city Evan turned to me, "You know what the partners will say when you bring up making a gift to the center?"

"Yeah, make a commitment and then pad our bill to make up for it. The Reverend Sam school of accounting."

"Exactly."

"Our contributions and any others we can garner will have to be how we handle this. You okay with that?"

"Yeah."

"You know, there are days when I think seriously about striking out on my own. Maybe after this campaign."

"Let me know."

XI

Somethin' for the Wife

D ressed in his best business suit, briefcase in one hand, suit bag slung over his shoulder, Charlie Givens rode down the escalator exiting O'Hare while trying to calm his anxiety that he was not worthy of his present assignment as he looked anxiously for Stanley Glick.

A group of ragtag looking drivers were at the next level, holding an array of name signs, some professional, others hastily scrawled, but no Stanley.

Today, July 8th, was a big deal. Glick was the recently elected chair of the Sessions University annual fund-raising campaign. As its newly appointed 28-year-old director, Charlie was to orient and brief Stanley on the fund's programming for the new fiscal year. Stanley, an alum, also served on the university's board of trustees and in real life was the chairman and CEO of Stein and Huntzinger, a haberdashery founded by relatives, now franchised nationwide.

Stanley was a likeable fellow who bore a slight resemblance to Rodney Dangerfield and who had taken a shine to Charlie, a big, enthusiastic man whose perfectly tailored suits graced his rotund frame. Funny thing about Stanley. With a gravelly, marble mouthed voice he could never get Charlie's name right. To Stanley Charlie was a slap on the back "Chaz". Charlie was fine with that. Stanley's approval, he felt, and some meaningful progress on this next year's annual fund was all that stood between him and getting fired.

He stood at the bottom of the escalator for some time. No Stanley. Then, reassuring himself that Stanley had happily volunteered to pick him up at the airport, he went out to the lanes of traffic to see whether Stanley was there or whether he might be circling by. No Stanley. Then an idea came to him. He went back and looked more closely at the name signs the drivers were holding. Sure enough on one sign was scrawled, "Chaz Govans".

He walked up to the driver, "Did Mr. Glick send you?"

"Yeah. Said I was to tell you he got de-tained."

He was shocked when the driver led him to a stretch limousine, took his suit bag and put it in the trunk. Charlie preferred to keep his briefcase with him so he could review once again the report he was to give Stanley, a report that he had rehearsed with his wife, Janie, several times the previous day.

Surreptitiously, on their way to Highland Park, he took pictures of his surroundings with his iPhone and texted them to Janie - the TV on MSNBC, the fully stocked bar, the display of newspapers and magazines, a small coffee machine on a fold down shelf on the driver's front seat back, a bowl of fresh fruit, a vase with carnations all Velcro-ed into place, the various snack bags in a holder on the passenger's front seat back.

Eventually, they drove through a beautiful enclave neighborhood and the driver left him at a hedged, field stone mansion with a broad perfectly manicured front lawn sloping down to the street. He opened the wrought iron gate and walked up the rose lined flagstone stairs to the mahogany front door and self-consciously sounded the massive, polished solid brass rapper. At just about the time he was about to rap again with trepidation, the door swung open and Stanley was there dressed in casual slacks and a golfing shirt.

"Hey, Chaz," he said enthusiastically, stepping out into the sunlight, slapping him on the shoulder, "Good to see you. Hey, I had an idea. Let's go to the track!"

"The track?" Charlie felt his mind scrambling to comprehend what this meant. The track?

"Yeah. Time's ahwastin'. First race is about an hour from now."

Charlie's mind hit upon reality. Horse racing. "Uh, okay."

Stanley led him to the garage, pressed in a code and as door opened, turned to Charlie. "You drive."

It occurred to Charlie that Stanley was probably accustomed to being driven everywhere. He felt his stomach clench, felt sweat burst out on his upper lip and forehead. "Sure."

"Hey, take your suit jacket and tie off and put 'em in the back seat. No need for 'em. I promise not to look at the suitcoat's label. Might be one of our competitors. I'll get you some gift cards. We want you to look the best, right?"

Charlie put his briefcase and suit bag into the Cadillac's trunk and his suit coat and tie in the back seat and went around to the driver's side, adjusted the seat and the mirrors and very carefully backed the car out of the garage and down the driveway.

"So, how do we get there?"

"I don't know," Stanley told him unconcerned. "Use GPS."

So, Charlie laboriously typed in the name of the race-track and began the drive there while Stanley talked.

"Hey, sorry not to pick you up. Was on the phone with headquarters. You know, most of our line of clothing, men and women's, is made abroad, Taiwan, India, Mexico, you name it. Great savings but it creates a lotta communication issues. A lotta times I gotta step in and referee everybody pointin' fingers at everyone else. So, that's what was goin' down this mornin'. The details can kill you. A hem's off by an inch of even half inch and the product may not sell. Luckily these days we have great inventory control. You know how things work these days?"

"No, I don't."

"When someone buys an item in our store, the sale immediately goes into our inventory data base. So, if we do things right, we don't run out of inventory because that sale triggers the same item being made to replace the one just sold, and, more important, in theory at least we limit excess. Now we do have items that are duds and those just go on sale and we discontinue them. But tastes and demands change faster than you can believe so we always gotta be at the top of our game. Use focus groups to find out the latest trends, find the best price, find the best manufacturers to make the best quality items at the best cost. Moving target, always a challenge.

"But key, it's funny because I tell my great friend, your president, Dr. Mulligan (Charlie tried not to grimace. The president's name was Milliken.), that promoting Sessions University is not that much different from promoting a business. It's all a matter of quality, price, branding and reputation. You gotta have those if you want to succeed. I'm lucky. Our business has been around for a while. Great reputation. Same with the university. But then, there's one final thing for real success that is required above all."

"Yeah?"

"Personal trust. I not only gotta like you, which I do, Chaz, but I gotta believe in you. I gotta feel in my heart of hearts that you'd rather die than see the university, the annual fund, me and you fail. That's trust, baby, which is also why I like you, Chaz. You're the right guy for this job."

"Thanks so much," Charlie commented, smiling and beginning to relax a little bit. "I really appreciate that."

When they got to the track, Stanley reached into the glove box, pulled out a VIP parking pass and tossed it onto the top of the dash. They were waved in and directed up front. On the way into the stands, vendors were hawking programs, snacks, banners, jockey paraphernalia, miniature horse figurines and other items. Stanley pulled out a clip full of bills and bought an array of junk, handing each item to Charlie who was soon festooned and weighed down. He felt ridiculous. God, let it be certain that no one on the university staff could see him now.

"You always gotta look out for the little guy," Stanley told him as they entered the concourse. "I try to help these guys and gals out." He held out a hand, signaling to Charlie to stop and as folks walked by he gave many of the items away, particularly to one older gentleman trailing three grandchildren.

They took an elevator to the VIP Club on the third floor, a long semi-circular room with wall to ceiling glass, lined with dining tables facing a panoramic view of the track's deep brown loam, the stark white of the guard rail curving off into the distance, the emerald-green infield and the finish line. Quite impressive.

"Hey," Stanley told him, "We can order a quick lunch, scan the racing sheets for our bets on the first race and go bet before the windows close."

"Oh my God, Stanley, I can't bet on horse racing with the university's expense account money. Can you see me putting that on an expense report?"

"Ahhh, don' worry about it. We'll bet with house money."

"House money?"

"Yeah, I'll loan you some "up front whip out", as they used to say in tha 'hood, and in the end we can split the winnings minus your bets. Okay?"

"What if we don't win?"

"Don' worry about it. Now look, you know what a quinella is?"

"Haven't a clue." Charlie with a sinking feeling was beginning to feel way in over his head. Was he not here to give Stanley a report on this year's annual fund program? That seemed to be the last thing on Stanley's mind. How was he going to redirect the conversation back to the topic he was here to discuss? Well, they had the rest of the day. He would just have to go with the flow and look for the right opportunity. He felt a spasm of panic as he imagined having to return to the university and report that he had failed in his mission. What would his boss and colleagues think and, worse, say, if they found out how he was spending his day with this board member? What would he say to Janie if he got canned?

"So, a quinella is when you bet on the first two horses to win or show, come in first or second. Doesn't matter which order they finish in. If those two horses win or show, you win! That's what I like to play."

A waiter came and they ordered sandwiches, pastrami and a Dr. Pepper for Stanley, a club and unsweetened iced tea for Charlie. As soon as the waiter left, Stanley said, "Ok, let's hustle. You got your two picks?"

"Yeah." Randomly, Charlie looked down and chose two horses, ignoring the daunting odds for both, "Numbers three and five, Willie's Lust and Cal Girl."

"Ok, I like one and six myself. Fairly decent odds, Jonny Cum Lately and Liar's Polka. Let's go."

They took the elevator down to the betting windows.

The line to the quinella window was short.

"Ok, let's see," Stanley told the ticket seller, as he pulled his money clip out of his back pocket and proffered a credit card from behind the wad of cash, "We'll take two hundred bucks on three and five and two hundred bucks on one and six." He pocketed the tickets and they headed back to the VIP Club.

Charlie was thinking to himself, "Two hundred bucks! How many races are there? Seven! How would I ever pay him back? Awww, shit. What would Janie say if I show up and had lost a thousand or two thousand at the race track and owed a debt to a board member? Holy shit. What the hell am I going to do?" He felt as if the entire situation, the entire day, his entire purpose in being had gone totally rogue. What the hell was he going to do?

They were just starting their sandwiches when the first race launched. They watched eagerly as the horses rounded the far corner of the track and disappeared down the straightaway at the other side. Then they listened expectantly as the announcer summarized the horses' progress. Damned if number three and five were in the group of leading horses. The horses came storming around the corner toward the finish line.

Stanley stood, turned to him, slapped him so hard on the back that he almost blew out a mouthful of his sandwich and yelled, "Hey, look at your damn horses. They're winnin'!"

Charlie stood and watched and grew increasingly elated. He began to jump up and down and root for them as did Stanley. They were like two twelve-year-olds. And damned, his two horses came in first and second, win and show.

"You won! You won!" Stanley shouted at him. "God damn it, Charlie. You won!" Jumping up and down, they hugged.

"Holy shit, Stanley. I won!"

"You won over two thousand bucks, buddy! Way to go. I told you you were a winner."

Charlie looked around. Clearly, he and Stanley were amusing the other patrons. He cooled his reaction immediately, now embarrassed.

They figured out their next bets, went down to the betting windows and Stanley cashed in Charlie's ticket, put the wad of bills into his pants pocket, pulled out his clip and charged the next round. And so it went for the rest of the afternoon, Stanley placing Charlie's winnings in the middle of their table and paying for their betting with his card. And they had a wonderful, animated time losing every race for the rest of the day.

When they stood to leave, Stanley picked up the wad of Charlie's winnings and handed it to him.

Charlie was stunned. He looked at Stanley, "But I

thought we were subtracting my bets and splitting the remainder?"

Stanley waved a hand, "Ahhh, keep it, Chaz. Gotta take somethin' home for the wife. Send her some nice flowers or get her a nice gift. Pays off in the bedroom."

"Jesus, Stanley."

XII

Race Day

| ADAPTED FROM *Danced by the Light of the Moon* |

The two Hoffer 43 sloops were anchored and rafted off the British Virgin Islands' Jost Van Dyke when vacation tour leader and captain, Ramsey Flynn, standing at *Kestrel's* stern pulpit, adjusted his small scotch-colored glasses, smoothed his wavy white hair and announced with vigorous enthusiasm to its crew and to those on sister ship, *Clockwork*, "Today! Is our race day!"

His bonhomie optimism had undoubtedly been used in his prior vocation when posting junior State Department personnel to woebegone third world assignments.

The crews on both boats, nursing hangovers from the night before at Foxy's, having risen to an overcast and blustery morning, did not comment. Full of excitement on their first day in the islands they had indeed agreed to race on day three, the losing crew buying the winning crew dinner.

On *Clockwork* were Gail Irwin, a sailing instructor at Magothy College and co-captain of *Clockwork*, single and searching, Jeff and Sally Bernard, Chesapeake Bay recreational sailors in need of a vacation from inside-the-Beltway work stress, Mark Berger, an ace Marblehead,

Massachusetts raised sailor, a runty, agile fellow with a large orange mustache and sideburns, black curly hair, bushy eyebrows and thick glasses, a kind of Jewish Yosemite Sam, a commodities trader, interested in Gail who on no uncertain terms had slapped down any possibility and Mary and Hugh McFeeley, PhDs, new to sailing, hoping for an adventure vacation.

On Ramsey's boat *Kestrel* were his granddaughter, Alicia, a sophomore at Georgetown, her boyfriend, Abdullah, and Patricia Reeder, Ramsey's younger girlfriend.

An inveterate sailor, Flynn was the perfect picture of the State Department retiree – well-groomed and well fed, costumed in a rugby striped Izod shirt, huge sailing shorts, sea anchor belt and canvas docksiders.

Several times annually he organized bareboat charters and other vacations among friends and acquaintances. For his efforts and the accompanying quality and cost savings enjoyed by his fellow travelers, he and a companion traveled at no cost.

On this trip they had arrived on St. Thomas and made their way to their charter company only to discover that *Clockwork* had electrical problems and was being worked on in her slip and that neither it nor *Kestrel* had been made up and were not ready to sail. In the end they had left the next morning after a charter company expense paid party in St. Thomas. Ramsey had adjusted their itinerary accordingly, leaving them to wonder whether the charter company had been selected based on a sweetheart deal rather than quality of boats, equipment and service.

Anchored nearby was a forty-foot ocean going

trimaran, *Calypso,* piloted by the French vagabond, Jean Claude, whom Gail had picked up at their St. Thomas party. Late the night before Jeff and Sally had spied Gail swimming in the moonlight over to *Calypso.*

Ramsey prattled on, ignoring their paralysis.

"This morning, we'll motor out into the Caribbean Sea toward the mid-point between Jost Van Dyke and Tortola, hoist sails and set a course on a close starboard reach. This will take us past Tortola and then Guana and Great Camanoe Islands. At that point we'll make a tack to port and sail onto Virgin Gorda. While we'll have a bit of exposure to open waters doing this, it's a much better course than if we were to go back through the Sir Francis Drake Channel where there would be a heavy tide against us as well as headwinds. By sailing this course, we avoid all that. In fact, we set ourselves up for using the Channel's tide and the prevailing Easterlies in our favor all the way on our return."

Gail spoke to the crew of *Clockwork,* "We're going to wait an hour while everyone has breakfast, stokes up on various antacids, headache remedies and vitamins and gets organized and then we'll motor out together."

"You know," Jeff told her, "It's not exactly a great day for a race."

"Let's just try for some efficient sailing and let everything else take care of itself."

The noise of Jean Claude's anchor chain being winched abroad caused them to look his way

Jean Claude, a lithe, bearded and deeply tanned figure with long nut-brown hair streaming behind him, was at the bow. He fastened the anchor with a few sharp movements and with speed and dexterity made his way back to the cockpit. The breeze was already bearing Calypso off when he began winching out his main sail from the mast. The boat fell off further, then out came his roller furled jib. He took the wheel, righted the boat, jibed and sailed in a wide circle then came speeding up from their sterns. He slowed as he winched his sails back in so that he came to a stop directly beside *Clockwork* and tossed them lines, then fenders, helping to secure the two boats one to the other.

Berger looked at the rest of them sitting in *Clockwork's* cockpit. He shook his head, "Friggin' amazin'. Farst class," he remarked in his Boston accent. "He is one god damned gifted Frog. Sails that thing like a fighter pilot. Top Gun."

Jean Claude jumped over Clockwork's lifelines onto her deck, winking at Gail as he did so. She turned away, ignoring him. "Ah *mes amis*, might I join you for, how you say, break fast?"

"Sure," Jeff told him, "Come on."

Mary McFealey, a tall, rounded woman with a kind, plain face said, "Hugh's fixing breakfast. He's a wonderful cook. Before that he was playing with the radio, listening to weather reports." Clearly, she and Hugh with her direction were trying to compensate for their inexperience.

Hugh's head emerged from inside the cabin. It was massive head with chiseled features, wild hair and metal spectacles, matched by a proportionate body, Albert Einstein as a tight end. Moving robotically, the sun glinting off his square wire rim glasses, he placed a plate full of scrambled eggs on the cockpit deck, then came paper plates and utensils, toasted muffins, butter and jam, a pot of coffee, then mugs.

As he came out to join them, he said in his flat, mechanical voice to no one in particular, "The weather forecast calls for rising winds and squalls throughout the afternoon, seas of six to eight feet and deteriorating conditions into the evening with gradual clearing overnight."

They all looked at him, concern on each of their faces.

"Hey," Jean Claude exclaimed, as he helped himself to breakfast, "Today is the grande race, is it not?"

"Yeah," Berger said, "We've had nothing but trouble with this boat from day one. I think Ramsey may have paid off the yard to sabotage us."

Clockwork had indeed thrown challenges at them each day, the engine conking out unexpected as they traveled though a current filled cut, the jib's roller furling releasing spontaneously as they were hit by a large gust of wind, the mainsail snagging in its track. What next, they wondered. The whole experience served to undermine their confidence in today's race plan.

"I don't think he had to pay them a damn thing," Sally observed. "Clearly, their incompetency did the work for him."

"Yeah..." Jeff laughed ruefully.

"Ah, you probably right. What do the beautiful captain think?"

Gail was clearly unhappy with the present conversation. "One step at a time. Let's see how things go."

"Ah. I can see why you are a good captain."

After breakfast, they straightened and stowed below, readied *Clockwork*'s deck and cabin and snacked on the remnants of breakfast to provide a *post-mortem* blotter for their digestive systems. Jean Claude bid them adieu to go into Roadtown for provisions. "*Je vous souhaite le meilleur*," he shouted to them over his shoulder as the wind filled *Calypso's* sails and he pulled away.

On the hour they released their rafting lines with *Kestrel* and followed her out into the Caribbean Sea.

A heavy 25 knot easterly was roiling the open sea, which met them with five-foot swells. They set their course, following *Kestrel*.

They watched as *Kestrel* turned into the wind and bucking up and down unfurled her sails as they brought them in tight then headed northeast on a close haul. In the haze caused by the heavy seas Tortola was on their starboard as a large green land mass at a good distance while Jost van Dyke faded rapidly aft. They were rocking and rolling on the waves, holding onto whatever grab rail or safety line was at hand.

"We'll stay on the same course for the next several hours," Gail told them.

"Jeff and Mark," Gail commanded, "Let's hoist the main and then the jib. Go for it!"

Gail headed them into the wind as Berger and Jeff struggled with the main. The wind picked up as they headed into it, whistling and whipping around them while the heavy black-green seas rolled under them, tossing the bow up and down dramatically so that the boat went crashing to the bottom of each trough and sent cascades of water over the decks and soaked them in the cockpit.

Suddenly they were wet and cool to the point of unpleasantness, the smell of sea water heavy around them and in their clothing.

The sail inched out slowly and thrashed around more

and more agitatedly. Berger climbed onto the cabin top and while the boat careened helped guide the main through its boom track while Jeff cranked on the winch. Finally, they had the main out.

"Okay, Sally, tighten the main sheet and the boom vang. Guys, let the jib out."

Berger pulled on the jib sheet while Jeff released the roller furling line. When the sail was out, they winched it tight and tied off its line.

"Nice wark," Berger said.

"You got it, *compadre*," Jeff replied.

The wind gusted suddenly as Gail changed their course to close hauled. They clutched hand holds, winches and lifelines and braced themselves against the cabin and the cockpit to prevent themselves from falling.

"Damnnnn," Gail shouted as she struggled mightily to keep the boat on course.

The boat plunged up and down over what seemed like larger and larger waves which sent great bursts of water over the bow and sprayed all of them with salt water again.

"Uh, Gail," Berger said slowly.

"Yeah?"

"Look at the tack of the jib, about three feet above it."

They all looked to where the jib was fastened at the very front of the boat.

Along the front of the sail where it attached to its halyard was a fifteen-inch tear.

"God damn it!" Gail said loudly.

They stared at the tear in disbelief as *Clockwork* continued to plunge up and over each oncoming wave.

In front of them *Kestrel* was growing smaller, fading in

the mists of spray from the heavy wind and wave action across the water.

"What do you think happened?" Mary McFealey asked.

"Ah..." Berger shrugged, "Anything can cause that – a friggin' cotter pin or over time just the sail rubbing against the bow pulpit on a broad reach."

"The problem is," Gail added, "that in these seas with the stress on the sail, especially as we pound in the waves, the tear is just going to grow until the sail blows out all at once."

"We could always tape it," said Jeff.

"Yeah, except I do not recall there being any tape on board when I did my inventory," Berger observed.

"Yeah, come to think of it, I didn't see any either."

"Plus the seas don't really recommend that I let either of you guys go out there," said Gail. "Even if we rig a safety line and you wear life jackets and I go downwind, it's still risky. I mean, this is a cruise guys, not really a race. Safety first."

As she spoke the bow came down hard and the seas coursed up into the jib and over the boat and they could see that it had caused the rip to grow another several inches.

"Mark and Jeff, let's roll in the jib well past the tear," Gail said. "I'll still try a long reach out into open water. We just won't go as fast or point as high. Mary, go below and get Ramsey on the VHF like I showed you how to do on our first day here.

"Sally, pull in the dinghy really tightly so that its bow is partially lifted. I don't want to chance it filling up with water in all this surf."

Once they had the jib rolled in past the tear and the

dinghy tied in more tightly, they listened as Mary repeatedly called Ramsey, "*Kestrel, Kestrel, Kestrel*, this is *Clockwork*. Come in, please..."

Finally, Mary said from below, a small quaver in her voice, "I can't get him, Gail.... No one's answering. It's like the radio's dead."

"Damn him," said Gail. "They probably forgot to turn on their radio or it accidentally got set to Hailer or something. We just talked about the importance of keeping contact today.... Try them a couple more times. We're probably out of cell phone range out here."

The winds continued to build and soon their wind gauge read thirty knots with gusts to thirty-five. The waves grew to where they were taking a real pounding going upwind and not making any significant progress. They were soaked to their skins and beginning to get cold.

They were silent for a while, watching the place on the horizon where *Kestrel* grew smaller by the moment.

Finally, Berger said, "Hey, Gail, no offense, but I think we're screwed."

Gail looked at the jib, at the main and at *Kestrel*, now a speck on the horizon. She sighed, "Yeah, you're right."

"Didn't help to have bad equipment," Jeff added.

They heard a sudden groan from below. Mary McFealey came stumbling out of the cockpit, threw herself at the lifeline on the low rail of the boat and vomited over the side.

"Oh, jeez," Gail rolled her eyes, "Okay, gang, let's completely roll in the jib. We aren't even going to be able to motor or motor sail in this crap without getting everyone sick."

"Really?" Jeff said, and they could tell he was still holding out some hope of closing the gap.

"Yeah, Jeff, we can't catch him. We don't need a sick crew. Worse we'll be motoring for the next five to seven hours directly into this swell. So, we'd just be beaten up, seasick and or worse, given this boat and its condition.

"If we head back into the Channel, we'll be in protected waters. We'll have to motor sail most of the way, given the current and the prevailing winds. But we can have lunch at Norman Island in the Bight, then head onto Virgin Gorda; be there by sunset in time for them to rub it in.

"Sally, go below and into the cabinet over the stove and get six garbage bags."

"Gail... garbage bags?" Sally asked her.

"Yeah, a trick I learned in the Mediterranean. Instant rain gear."

"Oh, boy," said Berger, "We're gonna look the part on this gahrbage cruise."

"Yeah, sweetie, you in particular."

"No comment. Don't want to get hit with a belaying pin by Capt' Bligh here."

They set about the business of getting Mary straightened away while Jeff and Berger completed the task of furling the jib after Gail started the engine and put the boat back into the wind. Sally handed out the garbage bags, which they poked holes into for their heads and arms. They instructed Mary to sit near the cabin entrance out of the way of the main traveler to keep her as much as possible in the center part of the boat.

"Well, don't we all look jus' fi-yahn!" Gail said in a Southern accent, surveying her garbage bag clad crew.

"No cameras!" said Jeff.

Ordinarily someone would have dashed below for a camera; under the circumstances, no one moved.

When the jib was in and the main trimmed, Gail put them through a port tack and fell off into a broad reach with the main out and the wind behind them helped by the engine.

"We're going through Thatch Island Cut and into the Sir Francis Drake Channel," Gail told them.

They moved with good speed on the much quieter broad reach, rolling heavily with the swell, toward the end of Tortola which loomed up on their port.

"Sally," Gail said, "you take the wheel for a couple minutes, just keep us on our present course; let me see whether we can call Ramsey and inform him of our situation. You'd think by now he'd wake up to the fact that something was going on and turn on his radio. The jerk."

In a moment they heard Gail trying futilely to raise *Kestrel* from what now seemed to be its position on the other side of the planet.

After what seemed a long period, she climbed out of the cabin, shaking her head, saying, "That's funny. I can't raise him on the radio. I wonder what the hell's going on. Could be bad reception. I don't know. It's like there's no damn reception or transmission. Tried him on my cell phone too – weak signal. The call wouldn't go through."

The inability to communicate with their tour leader did not sit well with the crew, particularly Jeff.

"Great display of leadership," he commented. "When the going gets tough, the tour leader disappears."

They made their way along Tortola and rounding up

traveled through the Cut, Great Thatch Island and Tortola tantalizingly close on each side. The smell of pork barbecue reached them from the beach.

"Gail, couldn't we stop in for a gin and tonic or something?" Berger asked.

"Tell you what," she told him, "I'll buy you a couple this evening."

"Done deal."

"Okay, be ready for some uphill climbing when we hit the Channel. We're going to have the wind and the tide against us."

As they cleared Little Thatch Island, the winds picked up and they headed up the Channel close hauled using the main and the engine.

The skies became more overcast, a dull, light gray, and visibility declined as the winds kept increasing. The seas in front and around them became a dark cobalt blue.

Gail increased the engine speed and they bucked up and down against the current, the steep chop and the wind, making very slow progress.

"We're headed toward Norman Island," Gail told them. "There's a very protected anchorage there called The Bight – which Robert Louis Stevenson wrote about in *Treasure Island* – where there is a real pirates' cave. We can anchor, regroup and have lunch."

The winds continued to increase and in front of them a black-grey squall line gradually formed. Rogue waves in seas unsettled by tide, wind and land mass kept colliding with them at odd angles throwing water up and into the cockpit. Sally looked at the goose bumps and pale skin on her arm as she reflected uneasily on the rivulets of sea water working their way into her already wet clothing.

Everyone was quiet, lost contemplatively in their own small state of concern bordering on misery.

"Gail, I do not like the look of this," Berger said evenly.

"Yeah," she said.

"If you get tired at the helm, let Jeff or me know."

"Sure."

As they watched, the squall hardened into a black line of clouds that gathered and then raced toward them as the wind picked up and then in an instant they were pelted with blinding cold rain. Their visibility vanished as if someone had turned a switch.

"Gusting forty plus friggin' knots," Gail told them.

She kept her compass course and they all held on as *Clockwork* bucked and heaved through heavier seas. The wind threw roundhouse punches at the main and the diesel clattered on obliviously as the seas washed over the bow, down the deck and into the cockpit and over them, trickling into the few remaining private places still dry and gurgling down the scuppers.

Eventually the squall passed and the skies lifted only to reveal another squall line in the distance, Tortola an indistinct landmass behind them, Norman Island a low black lump in front.

"We're not making a whole lot of progress," Berger commented, his mustache and sideburns full of water droplets, his glasses covered with them.

"Yeah," said Gail. "About what I expected. Would've been a whole lot worse on the outside passage with no place to hide."

They sat in place, holding on to railings, winches and lifelines, fatigued but on edge as the next squall bore down on them.

Once more they were pelted by heavy rain and winds. Visibility disappeared as they staggered along. Mary became sick again, crawling over to the leeward side of the boat and puking quietly over the rail.

The skies lifted only to reveal another squall line and a slightly closer Norman Island.

They were hit yet again by a third squall line before they rounded up into The Bight and anchored, Jeff and Berger handling the chores, rolling the main into the mast and then dropping the anchor while Gail backed the boat hard against the rode to assure the anchor had set firmly.

They were close in on the low cliff in The Bight near the famous cave.

Sally went down below and did her best to make turkey sandwiches and passed them up along with left over brie, crackers and soft drinks, the wind whistling and howling above as occasional spatters of rain were thrown against them.

Their mood improved as they ate, looking around at the wet greenery of the island, at the sea breaking on shore and at the anchorage where there were only two other boats, obviously waiting out the storm. The impressively large high ceiling entrance of the cave stared back at them blankly and on any other day would have inspired exploration.

"Okay, everyone," Gail said when they had finished lunch and stowed their provisions, "Let's move on.... Mary are you feeling better?"

"Oh... a hundred per cent, Gail. Thanks everyone for helping me over that rough spot."

"You're welcome," the majority of them said in unison.

"Let's motor out," said Gail, "and not bother to winch out the main sail. I'm not sure it's going to do us a whole lot of good on the course we want directly down the Channel."

They raised the anchor without complication and motored out from behind the island only to glimpse unhappily at yet another squall line bearing down on them.

"Jesus H. Christ," Gail said matter-of-factly. "While there is still some visibility, you'll see Peter Island on our starboard over there. We'll likely stop there on our way back. Today, obviously, we just want to make tracks to Virgin Gorda."

The squall line descended upon them with drenching and pelting rain and heavy gusting winds. They held on as best they could, each of them in their own small place where they had been riding out the storm the whole day and knew what to hold on to and when to turn away from the waves.

When the skies cleared, they could see Peter Island now on their beam as they headed up the Channel directly into the wind, the boat rolling up and over one wave only to crash into the next, crawling against the wind and tide, the squall line in the distance.

As they descended a wave, the engine suddenly revved higher and freely, as if the transmission had suddenly been pulled out of gear.

Their momentum slowed and they began drifting off course to port, being pushed aside by oncoming waves as if they were standing in the way.

"Now that's weird," said Gail, puzzled.

She reached to the throttle control on the right side of the steering pedestal and pushed it forward. The engine revved freely with no effect. She reached over to the left and pulled the transmission gear selector to neutral and then put it back into forward and pushed the throttle. The engine again revved freely. She put the transmission in reverse. Same result.

"Damn, I've never had this happen before."

They all looking at one another.

"Hey, Jeff, check out the transmission linkage."

"Sure." Jeff leaned over, opened the lazarette and stuck his head into the hold, looking for where the transmission linkage was routed out of the pedestal to the transmission. He climbed in to get a better look while Sally held the lid so it would not slam shut on him.

He stuck his head out a few moments later. "Everything's hooked up, just like it should be."

"Okay," said Gail quietly, clearly puzzled. In reflex she turned the wheel to starboard. A look of alarm crossed her features. "God damn it!" she said, "I barely have steering. Look!" She moved the wheel back and forth. There were a few inches of play to either side, but that was it. "What in the hell is going on here.... Roll out the main!"

Berger scrambled to the cabin top to guide the main along its track while Jeff cranked it. Gradually, with great flailing, it was out.

The heavy winds caught the main and they slid into a beam reach. Roadtown, on Tortola, was directly in front of them but as they made headway they were also sliding toward the west end of Tortola where it curved from

Roadtown and wrapped partially around the channel. The squall line bore in on them and visibility disappeared again as they were pelted by more rain. Their garbage bag rain gear was becoming all but useless against the onslaught.

Berger clambered down from the top of the cabin as Jeff took the place in the cockpit he had occupied all morning.

"Just in time," Gail told them. "Nice work. Look, given where we are right now, our best bet is to stay on this course – not like we have a choice – and sail to Roadtown for repairs. It's directly in front of us on this same point of sail. The issue is whether we can maintain this point because I can't steer us much of anyplace else, plus we've got the wind, the waves and the tide pushing us down the Channel. We can contact Ramsey and the charter company from there. This boat's pretty much done for I think."

"Great," said Jeff. They all looked at each other with resignation and despair.

The squall passed but the winds picked up again, 35 on the wind gauge, gusting to 40, to the point they were being knocked over.

Berger and Jeff worked the main sheet, spilling air from the main as the winds gusted to help them from being overpowered but trying to maintain enough drive to keep them on the reach.

Gail began to look increasingly worried as *Clockwork* slid down the Channel and made only moderate progress toward Roadtown.

Finally she took a large breath and said, "Guys, this is not good. I can't steer, the wind, waves and tide are drifting us down the Channel. If this keeps up, we can't make

Roadtown and we'll keep drifting like this right onto the rocks on the leeward shore of Tortola."

They looked off into the distance. On their port side the island was looming ever larger.

"Jeff, why don't you and Hugh try the auxiliary tiller," Gail said with increasing fear in her voice. "There's a brass access plate behind me. Look around for the tiller."

Jeff found the tiller in amongst a nest of line where it had fallen from its holder, while Berger examined the access plate on top of the transom and discovered it required a special tool.

"Ho-kay," he said, looking at Gail for confirmation.

Gail said, "Mary, Hugh, Sally. Can you guys go below and look for what's probably about a three-to-six-inch tool, probably has a T-handle and a hexagonal fitting at the end."

Over the course of the next five minutes they searched every drawer and every cabinet, locker and lazarette and turned up nothing. Another squall line was in the distance, bearing down on them. The steep hills of Tortola grew on their port while they continued to make slow headway toward Roadtown, which slipped increasingly to their starboard.

"Well," said Berger, "we'll just unscrew the whole fitting. See whether you guys can find a Phillips head screwdriver.

"There's nothing," said Jeff, "not a tool on this boat."

Berger laughed. "Well, what else would we expect. Great charter service Ramsey's hooked us up with."

"Hey," Jeff said, "let me get down in the hold and get a better look at what's going on with the transmission linkage and the steering assembly. Maybe I can just hand shift the sucker, if there's a linkage problem, or maybe some belt's slipped off or broken on the steering."

"Good idea," Gail told him.

He opened the lazarette again, "Then we'll just get the hell out of here.... Open the other side so I can get some more light."

Mary McFealey opened and held the opposite lazarette lid.

His voice came from the hold, "Shift to forward, then back to neutral and then back to reverse."

Gail followed his instructions as the engine clattered away without effect.

There was silence for a time, save for light cursing as Jeff bent in unfamiliar positions. The wind picked up mightily and the new squall came at them as *Clockwork* bucked along. A very unpleasant feeling crept into Sally's stomach.

From below, Jeff's voice came to them faintly, an awe-struck, "Ohhhhh shit!"

Berger yelled at him, "What the hell's goin' on?!"

Jeff was silent, obviously still grappling with the situation.

Then he stood up in the hold and faced them, pale and grim, "The reason," he told Gail, "you've got no drive is that the drive shaft has broken, a couple inches from the coupling. The shaft has drifted out so that there's only about two inches of it left in the boat. I tried to pull it back in and I couldn't. It's stuck."

"Oh, Jesus... it's stuck all right," Gail replied, "on the rudder. It's drifted out and bound itself there, which is why we have almost no steering."

"Jeff," said Gail, "Get back up here. We're going to need all hands on deck"

"Mary, I think we'd better call for help on the radio. You feel well enough to do that?"

Mary looked uncertain, "Sure, but how do I do that?"

"You simply get on Channel 16 and put out a call for assistance. Say that we have a broken shaft that is bound on our rudder; that we're in the center of the Sir Francis Drake channel drifting toward the rocks on the shore of Tortola at the end of the channel. Request a tow, then try to call Ramsey and inform him of our situation."

"What about the Coast Guard?" asked Jeff.

"No such thing in the Virgin Islands."

"Jesus..."

Mary went below and they could hear faintly over the roar of the storm snatches of her calling on radio.

The rains descended on them again, the boat heeled over and in the gray Jeff and Berger worked the main. They could feel the current and the wind pushing and pulling them toward Tortola.

Mary emerged from the cabin. "No one's answering!" she said. Her lips quivered and a small tear drifted down her face.

"Damn it," said Gail, "Great. Sally, go into my bag and get my cell phone, will you?"

Sally went below, located Gail's bag, found the cell phone in a zip lock bag and returned with it to the cockpit.

Gail shielded herself from the elements as best she could, pressed her speed dial for Ramsey's phone and listened intently.

She sighed, "Nothing.... I've got almost no signal; he

probably has even less where he is. I know he has his on –
we agreed to that.... I'll try the charter company."

She hit her speed dial again and listened for a response.
"No," she said, "Same deal. I don't have any signal."

She looked up to the crew. "Okay, folks, for safety's
sake, we'd all better get life jackets on. Sally, you and Mary
go below and hand them out. Mark, you and I get the ones
that are equipped for safety line rings in case we have to
go to the bow in this mess. Sally, also bring up the safety
lines – they look like moving or towing straps with clips
on them - for Mark and I to clip into just in case. Jeff and
Mark, get the extra anchor and rode. If we continue on
this course, we can drop both anchors and hope they
keep us off the rocks."

Slowly, as they pulled life jackets from lockers below,
an overwhelming sad and panicky feeling came over
them – this was no dream, they were in real peril.

"Mary," Gail commanded once they had all put on their
life jackets, "Get on the radio and try to raise Ramsey one
more time and then try the charter company. We'll at least
exhaust every avenue of communication that we can."

Mary went below and Berger and Jeff climbed up from
the cabin looking grim.

Berger said, "Well, we found the extra anchar. I noted
that it was there on our inspection, but missed that it's
tangled up in a Gahrdian knot of rode that's so bad that it
would take an hour or two to get it free. Frankly, I think
you might have to cut the damn thing out."

"Peachy," Gail remarked.

"There's no answer!" Mary shouted up. "No one's
answering us!"

"Maybe we're out of range," Jeff said.

Gail grimaced but made no reply.

The squall passed and they could see the shore of Tortola and rock outcroppings to their port. The hills stood out in great detail, a road by the shoreline, rock outcroppings amongst the trees as the hills ascended into the low gray clouds.

Sally went back behind Gail and said into her ear, "Is this as bad a situation as I think it is?"

Gail fought to keep her balance as the boat shifted and a wave washed over them. "Worse," she spat out over her shoulder. "The wind, tide and wave action will run us right up onto the rocks over there in a couple minutes. We've got to save this boat somehow."

"What about dropping the anchor?"

"I don't know. In this depth with this wind and sea, it probably won't hold. Plus going out on the bow in these seas and weather is a dangerous maneuver even with a safety line. I was thinking that we could drop a stern anchor first to slow us down but that's not an option now...."

Her running assessment brought her to a decision. "All right, Berger, you and me. Let's get up there and drop the anchor and hope it grabs on something before we go into the rocks. We'll take a safety line out with us and clip onto it once it's secured on the bow."

"Jeez," Berger said, his face tightening. "Okay.

"Jeff, you and Sally get the main wrapped back into the mast."

Once the main was in, Gail handed the wheel to Jeff and she and Berger secured a safety line on the starboard cleat and made their way out along the deck carefully, half crawling, holding onto the handrails on the top of the cabin and the lifeline on the windward side of the boat as it staggered and crashed up and down as the oncoming surf hit it broadside. Waves washed over them as they inched their way forward.

The shore of Tortola was now only several hundred yards away. They could see waves breaking on the rocks and very little beach between the outcroppings. A mini-van drove by on the road above the beach, children staring out at them from the back seat.

Once they had reached the bow pulpit, Gail and Berger secured the safety line and clipped on. They held onto the bow pulpit for a time, getting their bearings while getting pounded by waves.

Finally, as the boat came out of a wave they reached down and in a coordinated movement freed the brake. In the cockpit they could feel more than hear the rattle of the chain as the anchor dove toward the bottom.

Gail and Berger waited until all the rode had played out and then gradually, with waves continuing to wash over them, made their way back into the cockpit.

"Jesus," blubbered Berger his glasses covered with water droplets. "Don't wanta do THAT ever again."

"Oh yeah," added Gail, shaking herself off and unclipping herself from the safety line. "Okay, everyone, pray."

They all looked at her.

"I am fucking serious. That's all that's left."

As they continued to gape at her, a sudden vibration ran through *Clockwork*.

Gail gasped, "The anchor just caught on something. Holy shit!"

Another vibration ran through the boat followed by a

series of them and then suddenly *Clockwork* lurched and her stern began to swing toward the shore on Tortola.

The skies darkened again and the wind picked up, the rains descended and they were caught in large steep rolling and unsettled waves, so that they were being jerked around as if on some amusement ride. They struggled to keep their balance.

"I don't know how long this sucker will hold," Gail half shouted over the storm.

They sat looking at one another and out toward the shoreline, now invisible in the rain.

From the gray toward their starboard they heard a shout and in a moment the dull outline of another vessel appeared.

"Hey!" they heard a French accented voice shout, "Don't you guys know ANYTHING!!!??? "

"It's Jean Claude!" Mary shouted.

They looked through the rainy mists and after several seconds the form of *Calypso* appeared, and in several more seconds they could see Jean Claude in yellow rain gear standing in her cockpit.

"There are ROCKS over there!" he shouted at them, like they were fools.

"Oh, THANKS!" Gail yelled at him. "OUR JIB'S RIPPED, WE HAVE A BROKEN SHAFT, OUR PROP'S BOUND ON THE RUDDER AND OUR RADIO IS DEAD!!!!!!!!"

"Ahhh... I thought you were just being STOOPID! You have to abandon ship... now!"

"How did you know we were here?!" Gail.

"I follow you, of course, with my very powerful binoculars! You think I don't know you never going to make Virgin Gorda in that boat?!"

Gail for once had no reply; none of them had a reply. It was all too true.

Jean Claude shouted, "I will toss you a line, come around opposite your cockpit. Jump into my trampoline. Quickly! Your anchor will not likely hold in these conditions."

Calypso came hobby-horsing toward them in the high, irregular seas, its diesel working hard. Jean Claude turned her so that she was headed into the wind and surging up and down beside them. He threw them a line that Jeff dove for and trapped atop the cabin.

They wrapped his line around the starboard winch and brought the boats closer to one another but far enough away to avoid collision.

They watched as *Calypso's* port hull rose and fell in front of them, the trampoline between it and the center hull rising and falling with the irregular motion of the waves. It would be a difficult jump.

"Unfasten the starboard lifelines," Gail told them. This created an open space between their deck and *Calypso's* outlying hull.

Berger looked at them, "I'll go foist." He turned and in two steps launched himself into the air between the boats, coming down hard where the inside of *Calypso's* outlying hull joined the trampoline and somersaulting to a stop.

He stood and grinned at them, "Yeah! Piece of cake. Jeff, get your ass over here!"

Jeff stepped back to give himself more room for his launch and did an imitation of Berger except with a lower trajectory.

Berger caught him and his force caused them both to fall backwards onto the trampoline.

Once they had returned to their feet, Gail said, "I have an idea! Hugh, you launch Sally and then Mary from here onto the trampoline. I don't think they can jump that far. Time it so you toss them when the hull's on the way down."

In a moment Hugh had Sally by the top and bottom of the back of her life jacket and as she screamed he launched her into Berger and Jeff's arms, a procedure that worked far better than any of them had thought it might.

Then he grabbed Mary, a much larger presence.

She began to protest, "I don't know... Ohhhh...."

With a massive, Olympian heave Mary was thrown to the skies, hands and legs waving spasmodically in turning motions as she descended screaming onto Berger, Jeff and Sally and wiped them out onto the trampoline.

Jean Claude shouted at them, "Another squall is coming through! Hurry up, *mes amis!*"

They glanced to the East and sure enough a low black line of clouds was descending on them rapidly.

Hugh in his life jacket, rain covered spectacles, slipped as he launched. Berger, Jeff and Sally could see immediately that he would land short of the hull and they reached out as he came crashing into its side, grabbing onto his clothes and life jacket and pulling him onto the hull and then the trampoline. He stood awkwardly but looked no worse for wear.

"Thank you," he intoned in his expressionless voice.

As they turned to Gail, the squall descended upon them in heavy gusts of wind and blinding rain and suddenly *Clockwork* began slipping backwards toward the rocks on shore, taking *Calypso* with her. The anchor had let go.

They could barely make out Gail in the cockpit.

"Gail, *mon amant*, jump quickly!!" Jean Claude implored.

He revved *Calypso's* engine hard trying to pull both boats away from the shore but the added power simply began to bring the boats together. He pulled back on the throttle to avoid a collision.

She yelled at them, "I can't make it.... It's too late!"

As the speed of both boats heading toward the rocks increased, she ran to the starboard cleat, pulled a rigging knife from her pocket and quickly cut through the line between the boats. As the line parted, she looked at them forlornly.

"*Mon Amant! MON AMANT*!!!" Jean Claude yelled at her as she and *Clockwork* vanished into the storm.

For a few moments they looked into the space where she had disappeared and then Jean Claude, muttering in loud despair, accelerated away from the shore.

Sally and Jeff, Mary and Hugh and Berger made their way into *Calypso's* cockpit and stood dejectedly.

For a time they rode out the storm heading into the wind while looking back into the gloom behind them.

Then Jean Claude said, "Berger, you take the wheel. Stay on this heading. The engine is holding us in place against the wind and current. Let me get to the radio. My handheld VHF," he motioned to it clipped to the waist under his rain gear, "is impossible to hear in all this...."
He gestured at the tumult going on around them. His countenance was that of a beaten numbed man.

It occurred to Sally that he was going below so that they did not have to hear his conversations.

As Jean Claude went below, the muffled ugly sound of *Clockwork's* hull smashing into the rocks and its grinding on them with each new wave reached them through the torrents of wind and rain.

They looked at each other in disbelief, horror and uncertainty as each crunch sound of the hull brought home the reality of their vessel being wrecked and fear and questions about what had happened or was happening to Gail.

"God," said Jeff, "There's nothing we can do...."

"As she suggested, pray, maybe," said Berger.

"Hey guys, can it," Sally told them, seeing that any conversation was greatly upsetting Mary McFealey.

They nodded to Sally.

After a time, Jean Claude emerged. "I have alerted the charter company and Ramsey about this situation," he said stoically. "Of course, they are all quite shocked and upset.

"The charter company will help mount a rescue mission to find our friend and salvage the boat....

"I should get you and *Calypso* to protected waters. There is no more we can do here except pray that our mate, Gail, has somehow survived this great *catastrophe*. I have told the charter company that you will spend the night with me in Soper's Hole – we will be running out of daylight before I could get you to Charlotte Amalie. Tomorrow I will deliver you to the charter company. They will alert Ramsey and he and his crew will meet you there."

"Our cruise is OVER," Mary McFealey said beginning to

cry, "All our things are GONE. Gail... I'm so sad..." she broke down weeping. Sally went to her and put an arm around her shoulders.

As the squall passed and visibility returned, they could make out *Clockwork*. She had come to rest sideways on the rocks, listing toward shore, each new wave lifting her up like some bathtub toy and pounding her into oblivion. The dinghy still hung off the stern cleat. Upside down and striped of its engine, it flapped spasmodically with the motions of wind and waves and the boat. Gail was nowhere in sight. *Clockwork* grew smaller and smaller as they motored down the Sir Francis Drake Channel to safety.

About the Author

Nelson Cover is a former non-profit administrator and consultant whose clients included numerous colleges, universities, hospitals, medical centers and think tanks.

His prior works include his first novel, *Danced by the Light of the Moon* and the two novels of the Sessions University series, *From the Midst of Wickedness* and *A Matter of Circumstance*.

Today, Cover resides in Vero Beach Florida where he continues his non-profit involvement with performing arts, social service, environmental and animal welfare groups.